688

By

New York Times Bestselling Author

ROBBIE WOLIVER

DEDICATION

To Marilyn, always.

And to every hardworking organization helping the immigrants—children and adults—at the U.S. Southern border.

Something weird is going on in Apartment *688*.
A novel-in-flash told in chapters of exactly 688 words each.*
*(Hyphenated and em-dashed words count as one word.)

Special thanks to Kenny Herzog, Claudia Justeson, Michael Martino, Randy Mastronicola, Audrey Pavia, Silvia M. Rey-Buzzonetti, Pia Savage, Catherine Schmoller and Jeanne Spellman for your assistance, feedback and/or edits. And to my workshop students, "Robbie's Writers," you've all inspired me.

Thank you: Cover design by Luis Rodriguez; cover photo by Marion Kahan

"Castaway," "There's a Spirit" and "Push and Pull": Lyrics by Robbie Woliver / Music by Nick Lohri ©2020

INTRODUCTION

In the past, my books included 1) a children's educational reading text 2) non-fiction subjects on children's health, a would-be murderess, and music history of Greenwich Village 3) a novel about a Deep Southern town called Creation.

I wanted to challenge myself to try something completely different. I thought I'd do so in a new novel incorporating elements of flash fiction. For those unfamiliar, flash fiction is a short fiction piece that's usually under 1,000 words. Sometimes as short as 10.

I recently discovered the novel-in-flash genre, where it is pretty much anything goes. At the time, I was five years into teaching a writing workshop series at the South Huntington Library on Long Island, NY, and I kept picking up more and more talented writers along the way. They became a well-bonded crew, "Robbie's Writers," whose work inspired me greatly. Out of all the styles we worked in, they seemed to get a kick out of flash fiction the most. Short and sweet. So, I figured that there must be something to it.

I decided to take this popular, new and unique style a step further, adding my take to the ever-evolving genre. Each chapter would be 688 words. Exactly.

What an exciting challenge that turned out to be. Not only did I have to get the important storytelling compacted, but also the editing. Every time I copyedited the story, I had to move all the word pieces around like a puzzle to come up with that magic number. 688. Proofreading was a bitch. But it was the most fun I ever had writing a book. The story behind why I chose 688 words is a bit more complicated than what you'll learn in the book, but please feel free to contact me to get the real story. I love telling it.

The other thing I wanted to do with this story was break some conventions. Besides the simple fact of me having to give in to my OCD and having an exact amount of words in each chapter, which I don't believe has ever been done before, I wanted each chapter to sort of live on its own—like a flash short story. I wanted a lot of interesting characters…like real life. I wanted the first section to be gloomy and rainy; the second to be hopeful and sunny; and the third…well, you'll see. So, it's stories within stories within sections within a bigger story.

There are also a few important themes I wanted to address. You'll discover them.

Jump to quarantine. A perfect time for a final edit on this book that I've been living with for two years. And as I was editing this book, I started thinking—well, this is a fun read (it is), so instead of sending it out and waiting what would probably be at least a year to get it published by a traditional publisher like my other books, why don't I just go to Amazon and get it published now. Give the people something even crazier than *Tiger King* to entertain them and occupy their time during their shelter-at-home lockdowns. My pandemic gift to you all

So that's what I've done.

I hope you enjoy it and I'd like to think this book will give you a healing laugh, chilling shiver or good cry, while taking your mind off the craziness of our current times.

This was much more fun than dealing with agents, publishers, editorial boards and non-existent marketing divisions.

Welcome to Lallie's world.
(Guess what? This section...exactly 688 words!)

PART ONE

RAIN

LALLIE

The TV flickers, casting shadows on her quilt Grandmother made.

It's past midnight and Lallie's head rests on her comfy goose-down pillow, under the smiling gazes of Sheldon Cooper and the *Game of Thrones* cast, on fading posters hanging loosely above her bed.

It's been a difficult day. Boss was a bitch. He found nothing good about her work today.

Lunch arrived late, and Boss glared at Lallie's cramped cubicle from his cavernous corner office (she could see his spectacular view of Central Park from her desk), waiting impatiently for her revised reports to be completed. She was hungry, but her beet salad arrived late, well past her half-hour lunchtime, and there was no way to eat now. With Boss watching.

Lallie, acid building in her empty stomach, punched out an hour and 17 minutes later than usual. There's no overtime here. All she wanted was to see Bill, take a warm bath, cuddle with her cat Sheldon, collapse into bed, and fall asleep watching *Broad City*.

The sudden rainstorm shot her with angry torrents of ice-cold pellets. Sure, this was the day she'd forego a coat. Spring, after all. Catching a ratty reflection of her mop of a new hairdo in the window of Viva, the spirited bar next-door to her soulless office, she cursed every damn cab after cab she missed. Uber wasn't her thing. Her brother drives an Uber, souring her already limited trust level. She so wanted to look nice for Bill who waits in the lobby at 6:15 for his daily dinner delivery. He doesn't trust dour Doorman. Something creepy about this new employ. Bill believed his food appeared tampered with whenever he'd trek to the lobby to pick up his take-out from this dicey hire with his indistinguishable tattoo crawling deviously up his neck, sneakily peeking out from his starched shirt collar, which was obviously just another annoyance to him. Bill knew Doorman thought, *This damn uniform*. He could tell by Doorman's ebony eyes that he was up to no good and he was not going to take any more chances with his food. So, Bill waits in the lobby for delivery, every evening, and is greeted by Lallie each day after work. They'd take the elevator together to the sixth floor, he to 689, she to 688. Bill thought she was cute; he might seriously date her. He just needed to clear up some business with Girlfriend first. And, yes, the rain ruined her hairdo, and yes, Bill was taken aback by her bedraggled appearance.

When Lallie enters the building, catching Bill's eye, he winces. Unlike Lallie, Girlfriend was radiant when wet. Their first kiss was in the rain.

Doorman glares. Lallie makes no eye contact with him. Bill has already informed her of his suspicions. Together, in the elevator, she apologizes for her appearance.

"No need. Rain'll do that," Bill says comfortingly, quite aware of the difference between Lallie in the rain and Girlfriend in the rain.

Bill's Curry Chicken (his usual Thursday order) smells so good, Lallie wishes he'd invite her to join him for dinner. But, of course, he doesn't. He never does. And anyway, she wanted a warm bath, Sheldon cuddles, her soft bed, and her inviting pillow to rest her head upon.

Broad City has been over by hours, but the TV rattles on. Lallie's head is resting on her comfy pillow. The rain slams her window. Her living room light is on. In her bathroom, Lallie's torso lay gently in the tub of scarlet water. The door to 688 is ajar, but Berde from 687, is preoccupied attending to Admiral Jackson, her blue-ribbon spaniel, who's suddenly become jittery passing Lallie's apartment. Distracted, Berde concentrates on buttoning his plaid coat, bending her head to his to reassure him, not seeing the slightly open door and Sheldon licking Curry Chicken off a paper plate lying on the kitchen floor. Once in the lobby, Berde complains to Admiral Jackson that it's 1 a.m. and damned Doorman's nowhere to be seen, and she has to hold the door for distraught Girlfriend, drenched, and in a blind rush to leave.

DAVEED

The final paycheck.

Daveed rips open the envelope, smiling broadly at the $688 check. He'd cash it first thing tomorrow. All he wants now is to lie back as best he can in his cramped bathtub—much shorter than his 6'3" frame. Knees up, he waves the paycheck back and forth. *I can get it now.*

Tomorrow he'll leave. Once again, unemployed, he fulfilled his mission. Earn enough to get to Texas and claim his child. Monica's family was already there, working with RAICES and Border Angels, to help gain asylum for his wife and daughter. Monica has a strong case. Her two brothers were killed by gangs back home in Guatemala, where Daveed is a wanted man.

Daveed arrived in New York City a year ago; easy to get lost there. Got work where he could, saved money, and hoped he'd be with Josefina by her third birthday last month. It was not to be. Border guards ripped her from Monica's arms, placing Monica in a Detention Center, and Josefina who knows where. Monica's sisters who have been living in the US for years, and are quite established, flew from their homes in LA, Iowa and Maryland to the Rio Grande Detention Center on the Texas-Mexico border to help secure Monica's release. But Josefina's fate is elsewhere. It's now time for Daveed to find her. He's clever and wily, and despite his years subsisting among Guatemalan gangs, he's never encountered an enemy like ICE. Fortunately, Angelica, Monica's oldest sister, has political clout and believes she found where Josefina might be.

However, nasty rumors swell around that place about kids being put up for adoption. How in the world could this happen, wonders a man who's seen the worst of humanity.

Things haven't been easy for Daveed. Back home in Escuintla, the crime capital of Guatemala, he associated with bad guys. It was the only way to survive. Three of Monica's brothers, Eddy, Osmin and Geovany, were members of the notorious Mara Salvatrucha gang. Rape, robbery, kidnappings, beheadings were the only way to survive in the moral and economic poverty where they scratched a bare existence. When Josefina arrived, Daveed knew it was time to rethink his lifestyle. It took him two years to leave Escuintla, get settled in America, and start saving to bring his family to safety. Monica's sisters already found their American Dream.

Monica and Josefina's trip north was perilous, even with Geovany accompanying them on the 50-day, 1,100-mile-plus trek. Walking ten hours a day. And this was better than *La Bestia*, the Beast, or Death Train, which Daveed endured when he took the dangerous journey. Eddy and Osmin didn't take the trip; they had been executed months before, for not taking part in their gang's attack on a local school.

Daveed felt guilty he was luxuriating in a warm bath.

With a succession of jobs—it was hard to hold on to employment with his mind so focused on his wife and daughter, and fear of ICE knocking at his door—he bounced from one menial position to the next with no more than a month's duration each, but savoring every small pittance of a paycheck he received. Off he was, dust in the wind, in the middle of the day or the dead of night, not to be caught and returned to the hellhole from which he so fortunately escaped.

Angelica was sure that when the whole family was reunited, she would be able to attain permanent legal status for all three of them.

But Daveed remains haunted by Escuintla. He's unsettled, unstable and perhaps even dangerous. He's been buzzed, and a bit out of his mind for days. These hard-earned savings would lead him to his dear Monica and hopefully Josefina. The mess he was leaving behind would remain like disturbed air, like the rainstorm outside his window.

He exits the tub, towels off, and packs his small bag of essentials, eager to leave his fleabag rental. But there's one last commitment. His appointment to get his gang tattoo lasered from his neck, for which he now, thankfully, has the $688 fee.

BOSS

Boss slumps down on the expensive leather couch. His short, his gigantic feet dangle.

Not the most comfortable place to land when exhausted, but it's the first piece of furniture to encounter in the colossal living room. Tired. Dead tired. Saturdays are like this. Dropping Chase at indoor soccer, Britt at dance class and Madison at Maddison's house for a playdate, it's all a chore.

"Why does our maid's brother deserve a $1,000 wedding gift?"

Tarly snarls, "She's worked for us for 12 years. She'll tell people we're cheap." Her obscenely large diamond studs glitter like raindrops for a second, as she storms out of the house.

He dreads watching TV. It was all over the news yesterday. Young woman found beheaded in her apartment, an employee of Harbinger Finance & Realty. Bad for business.

Footage of stupid Sandra, office manager, weeping. Of all 688 employees to choose from. The apartment building, cops entering and exiting like ants. A millennial interviewed about how sweet Lallie was. Photo of Lallie holding Sheldon. Odd, weepy Brother. Rain.

Boss paces, his $12,018 Salvatore Ferragamo's digging into the plush snow-white carpet. Sniggles, the family poodle, nuzzles Boss's leg, but Boss ignores him, pushing him aside with his $6,009 right shoe. It's Tarly's damned annoying dog. He would have put him down years ago, but the kids are attached to it. The last thing he needs is a bunch of whining kids crying about a dumb dog.

The news is onto the next story. A fire in some bodega.

Lallie. Pathetic, frantic at her little desk. Staring into space, or out my window at Central Park, or at me. Silly girl. On Thursday, she wasn't quite herself. Her work was sloppy. She couldn't look me in the eye. Her head was somewhere else.

Boss never feels remorse, but there's a twinge of *some thing*, recalling the stern talk he had with her prior to her clocking out for the day. It was late and he had no patience for anything but getting out of the office. Fuck them, all the workers, for finding a secluded area of Viva when he entered, not that he would have joined them or bought them drinks anyway. To the pounding jukebox, he lost himself in Dewar's after Dewar's. From the window, he watches soaking wet, mop-headed Lallie's vain attempts at securing a cab. He could have had his waiting car service take her home, he fleetingly thinks.

Damn, I have to go back out into this fucking rain to pick up Britt. Those goddamn dance moms, all eyeing me. They're divorced for a reason.

As Boss picks up the remote, there's an update about Lallie. Something about a missing Doorman. And a composite. Boss shudders, turns off the TV and walks to the bar to pour himself a drink. He thinks of Tarly. She was worth leaving Brenda for but she's sure a pain-in-the-ass.

He walks into the kitchen and sees the $1,000 check on the table, made out to Yaro and his new wife Be'Linda. Next to it is the contract for the sale of his house: One Diamond Circle, Oak Estates, Sands Point, Long Island: $14.2 million. Their move to Greenwich, Connecticut has been in the works for months. Tarly's idea.

But something else is bothering him. He calls Driver to pick up Britt, then Chase; Madison will be sleeping over at Maddison's.

He grabs an umbrella and walks outside to the guest house, a quaint sky-blue and lime Victorian that would serve as a mansion for any other family. He unlocks the door and in the upscale country kitchen he rapidly retrieves an envelope taped underneath the $40,000 Yaya & Wenge African-wood dining table and secrets it in his pocket. He locks up, clicks his remote to open the garage, and gets into the Porsche wagon. Tarly has the Bentley. Driver has the Mercedes.

He has many choices; Sands Point is surrounded by water. He drives to the Long Island Sound, exits his car, walks down the windy, sand-furled beach and in the whipping rain, throws Lallie's apartment key into the turbulent wet swirl.

GHOST

There's a Ghost in Apartment 688.

She watches the workmen as they tear down sheetrock and replace it, as they rip out bathroom fixtures and replace them, as they solemnly remove the bathtub, and replace it, floors restored, cabinets changed, everything they can do to make it…different.

Ghost is uneasy. Becoming a ghost is stressful enough, but all this physical change around her? It's just not fair.

She likes the realtor Matty Lynn. They could have been closer friends in the corporal world, she thinks. She sees Matty Lynn cry the first time she enters the apartment. Ghost hopes Matty Lynn rents it to the right person. A hard-working single girl, trying to make her way through the muddle of work and play. Maybe someone with a cat. Damn, she misses Sheldon. She hasn't learned to transport herself yet—like to Brother, who's adopted Sheldon. She wants Brother to know that although they aren't very close, she appreciates his TV tears. Wait'll she can transport herself.

There are a few people she'd like to find.

Lead Detective Gerarra, seems like a nice guy. He's searched the place up and down, in and out, every square inch, for clues.

Lallie's seen his notes: the hair fibers, the not-very-good composite drawing of Doorman, interview with Boss, photos of Bill, Berde and the other tenants.

There are 30 apartments here—lots of in-house suspects. Girlfriend, Brother, they're all in the file. Gerarra's suspicious of everyone, according to his notes and the conversations he's had with fellow detectives in the apartment. But they don't come by anymore.

It'll be lonely until Matty Lynn finally gets someone to move in. She's required to tell perspective tenants about the murder, but this is New York and cheap apartments are at a premium. Apt. 688 will go for $3,500 a month now that it's renovated. For a two bedroom, not bad.

I'll miss Gerarra. When I learn to transport, he'll be one of my first visits.

The rain is incessant and bothers Ghost even though she doesn't have to worry about her hair anymore. *It reminds me of my last miserable day alive. I can't wait to learn to knock and rattle. Groan, moan and flutter. I think I'll be able to do those things.*

Oh, wait.

Matty Lynn enters 688. Berde *happens* to be walking by and tries to peer in. Admiral Jackson yelps just like that night. Berde gets the creeps and departs, comforting Admiral Jackson. He misses Sheldon, too.

Matty Lynn is with a young couple: Tara and Stan. They're in their late 20s, like Lallie.

They look a bit apprehensive.

"It's OK, come in," Matty Lynn offers, warmly. They enter gingerly. They're holding hands.

"Oh, it's nice," Tara says, surprised.

"Yeah, really nice," Stan agrees, eyeing the newly furnished digs.

"Wow," says Tara.

"It's the best offer Harbinger Realty has had in a while," Matty Lynn says, with a broad, please-rent-please smile.

Lallie likes her. She always has.

The couple walk around. Examining the molding, windows, large amount of space.

"Any questions?" Matty Lynn asks guardedly. This is her first showing here.

Tara looks at Stan. Stan, back at Tara. Matty Lynn knows what they're thinking.

"The entire apartment's been reconstructed," she assures them. "But full disclosure. Nobody knows where the actual, uhm, murder occurred. But the bedroom's all redone, and the bathroom is all completely new."

"I like it, Stan, but I don't know."

"Listen, hon, you never know the full history when renting any apartment. At least Matty Lynn's been upfront with us."

"Did you know the girl?" Tara asks Matty Lynn.

"Yes, yes, I did," she answers. "She was very, very sweet. I didn't know her that well, she worked in the corporate office, but every time I met her, she was very sweet."

"I don't know," Tara says, "it's tragic and all, but every time I see her photo in the news, it gives me the creeps. She just looks creepy."

The sound of the bedroom light fixture crashing to the floor startles them all, Ghost included.

"Nahhhh," says Tara." I'm outta here."

Ghost. She's getting there.

GIRLFRIEND

She books the 2 a.m. flight to Gainesville.

Sitting in the terminal, Girlfriend furiously texts her cousin, Bernadette, a regional manager for Target.

She looks at the clock above the ticket booth and realizes she has some spare time, so she rushes into the ladies room to gather herself and repair her disheveled appearance. She stares at the mirror and reflects on this sudden turn of events. She also muses about how the wet look suits her. She seems to recall faintly that Bill told her that. Maybe it was after they kissed in the rain once.

She had only packed bare necessities, all suddenly, hurriedly. There isn't much to work with, and she's without assistants. She brushes her hair and dries it under the hand dryer. She applies some foundation, powder, eye liner, mascara and a pale new pink lipstick for which she is the spokesmodel.

Bernadette, newly widowed, was welcoming her with open arms. "Anything you need."

Girlfriend pops another Xanax, the fourth in the last three hours. She takes a deep, restorative breath.

She instinctively knew Bill would ultimately break up with her because of his busy schedule, general indifference or her skyrocketing celebrity. She would never have guessed that it would be another woman. And certainly not that weirdo stalker who lived in the next apartment to him.

Girlfriend's phone beeps. It's Agent.

"What's this crazy voicemail I got from you," Agent shouts. "You sounded hysterical."

"I'm fine. All problems solved, love."

"Where are you? You know that you have a shoot in Chelsea tomorrow."

"I can't make it. Sorry. I have a family emergency."

"Is everything OK?"

"Yes, everything's OK now. But I have to go to Gainesville. I'll be at my cousin's, Bernadette."

"But this shoot is for the cover of *Marie Claire*. The Cover. What are you doing?"

"I can't talk now. I'll call you later."

When Girlfriend first met Bill, he was a shy, struggling photographer and she was a confident neophyte model. They hit it off right away, an odd couple, "Like Marilyn Monroe and Arthur Miller," her snarky mother would comment.

As Girlfriend and Bill both became more famous in their fields, there continued an unexplained electrical current between them, a powerful attraction that just got stronger and stronger, until it began to burn itself out. At least on Bill's side. He became secretive, paranoid and reclusive.

Girlfriend knew about Lallie's evening elevator rides with Bill, and it never struck a false or jealous note for her. Mother would say, "After all, just look at her, and then at you." She did acknowledge often to Bill that she thought Lallie might be a bit strange, obsessive. Girlfriend wasn't jealous, just objective, in her subjective way. She knew Bill was drifting away in these recent weeks and she was trying everything in her power to save the relationship. Bill was her rock in her very unfocused world living in the camera's eye. She hoped it might be his work that was distracting him: he was assigned the *Sports Illustrated* cover layout this week and a *Vogue* feature with the Haddid sisters. Lots of pressure.

Then the phone call came.

"We need to talk," Bill said.

Girlfriend knew what that meant. She rushed to his apartment on Thursday night, and it was one frustration after another, not unlike Lallie's struggles during the day. It was pouring and Girlfriend was soaked to the bone. She couldn't get into the building because Doorman had gone MIA and wasn't there. A tenant who recognized her from last week's *O* Magazine cover let her in, and then reported back to Super about missing Doorman and the unattended door, so Super just left the door unlocked. When Girlfriend arrived on floor six, she knocked, knocked at Bill's door, but no answer. However, Berde came out of her apartment with Admiral Jackson and slyly pointed to Lallie's, and said, "Oh, Bill's in there. With her."

That's when Girlfriend snapped.

"Flight 688 to Jacksonville is now boarding at Gate B."

Girlfriend gathers her bags and makes her way to the Sunshine State, where it is currently storming.

WORKMAN

Ah, someone's at the door. Lock number one is turning. Now lock two. Unlocked. In walks the ray of sunshine, Matty Lynn.

Who's she with? wonders Ghost. *He's damn cute. Hell, why weren't guys like this in my apartment when I was alive? Probably looking to rent. I won't scare this one away.*

Poor Tara and Stan.

Oh, wait, he has a toolbox.

Matty Lynn points out the bedroom light fixture fragmented on the floor. Workman is here to fix it.

He turns off the electricity, plugs in his drill, clenches some screws in his teeth, sets up his ladder, carries the new light fixture under his arm, and up he climbs.

Cute tush, Ghost notices.

As Workman fiddles with the fixture, Ghost observes Matty Lynn's thumbs cirque-de Soleil'ing over her cellphone's keyboard. She's "liking" this. "Following" that. Instagramming an apartment on 24th Street. Scrolling. Texting. Acrobatic thumbs all aflutter. Probably rented 12 apartments in those three minutes.

Workman gets talkative. Matty Lynn's in no mood, but she's always polite. Her trademark: Sweet disposition.

"So, what's the story here," he asks. "Some chick got offed?"

"Yes, there was a murder. Her name was…is…Lallie."

"Is it true her head was chopped off and it was lying on her pillow and her body was in the bathtub?"

"Yes," Matty Lynn politely responds, her stomach turning even to this day at the thought of poor Lallie's demise.

"Man, is that so gross. What kind of sicko would do something like that?"

Damn Right, thinks Ghost.

"Yeah, they haven't found the killer," Matty Lynn says flatly.

"Did you know the chick?"'

Matty Lynn didn't quite hear the question. "Sorry, I didn't catch that."

He stops drilling. "Did you know the chick?"

"Yeah. I did."

"What was she like? Was she hot? Was it like a sex crime?"

Matty Lynn doesn't answer him; pretends she didn't hear.

"You have a picture of her?"

"I do."

"Can I see it?"

OK, Matty Lynn thinks, the more people who see her photo, the more she's in people's minds. Who knows, maybe he saw her on the street one day and can provide valuable information.

She finds the picture that the media has been using. Ghost *hates* that photo.

She raises her phone up to him, and he leans down to see it.

"Not what I expected," he says.

"What did you expect?"

"Someone cuter. Who'd bother with that? It must've been an old boyfriend she was hounding."

The sound of the ladder crashing to the floor causes Matty Lynn to skip a heartbeat or two. Workman is flat on his back, looking like the old-timey outlines cops drew around riddled bodies after a mob shootout, the ladder on top of him, drill whirring into his groin.

His screams of pain reverberate, echoing throughout the empty bedroom. Matty Lynn might have waited a few seconds longer than she should have before pulling the plug on the drill and moving the ladder off Workman. Between his moans, and sighs and groans (*Hey, that's my job*, Ghost mutters to herself), Matty Lynn instructs him to not move as she frantically calls 911. Not that he could, he is already paralyzed from the waist down. Spine snapped.

Matty Lynn does her best to console him, and in six minutes, the paramedics arrive at the door. They secure his neck, strap him in the stretcher and rush him to Roosevelt Hospital. Everyone gone, Matty Lynn sits on the bedroom floor legs crossed, arms wrapped around her chest, rocking back and forth.

"Asshole," she whispers out loud. She then looks toward the ladder, the new shattered fixture, back up at the light, and curiously scans the room.

Something unintelligible comes sputtering from deep within. Then, with more confidence she stands up and asks, "Lallie?"

She holds her breath. Nothing, of course. She giggles to herself, walks into the bathroom, splashes water on her face, puts on some blush and refreshes her lipstick, shakes out her hair, and walks toward the door.

"Bye, Lallie," she says with a chuckle.

As she turns the knob to exit, the ladder scrapes along the floor.

VIVA

Two weeks after viewing Lallie's place, Stan and Tara settle for a Bleecker Street studio as their first apartment together.

Helpful Matty Lynn found and negotiated the apartment for them, although Harbinger Finance & Realty exacted an excessive fee. It was difficult not to resent Harbinger, and for a New York-minute the apolitical couple felt like downtrodden Socialists battling bloodsucking landlords. Maybe more than a minute.

With a hefty $2,535 monthly rent, they're apartment-poor, but they're young and the future looks bright for them. That is until Stan was murdered.

It was the night of Tara's 27th birthday. They'd meet at Viva, where Matty Lynn was to buy them a congratulatory round, and then home. However, the weather was miserable, and Stan desperately needed the bathroom, so they decided to stay, eat some sliders and down some beers there, even though there was a palpable weird vibe in the muggy air. It had been raining for days, and it was affecting everyone's mood. There was a burst pipe in the men's room, closing it for the night; a scuffle broke out outside injuring three bouncers; battles erupted in the crowded ladies room, the only restroom available, with impatient patrons now peeing in sinks; and there were more than the usual mean drunks at the bar. The most unpleasant being Boss, whose scowl alone could set off a brawl. Girlfriend, fresh from her brief Floridian R&R, was there drinking off a failed audition held in a studio in the Harbinger Building next door, for an upcoming Netflix series about models in 1970s New York that she believed she aced.

"How could I blow that?" she cried to Agent afterwards.

The kitchen was also tension filled. Chef was in a most foul mood, taking his frustration out on the dishwashers, busboys and waitstaff, all who defied him at every turn. His prized Shun Classic Chef Knife went missing; customers were traipsing through the kitchen mistaking it for perhaps an employee's restroom.

Daveed started working there as a busboy a week prior, returning to New York without Monica and Josefina after three unproductive, torturous weeks in Texas. He is determined to keep his cool and this job because he's paying off debts Angelica is incurring on his behalf to aid Monica and find Josefina.

Daveed walks toward the bar, leaving the back-of-the-house chaos behind, and a bloodstained-footprint in his wake. Or is it ketchup? Plates and silverware need to be cleared, and that's his job now.

His blood runs cold as he spies Girlfriend returning from the ladies room, looking as nervous as before her Gainesville getaway. There's a burgundy footprint in her wake, too. She notices Daveed and thinks she recognizes him from somewhere. Modeling? He's sexy enough.

As he turns from her, she observes the scar on his neck where the gang tattoo once resided. I'd remember that scar, she thinks, dismissing him from her consciousness. He's a fucking busboy.

Trying to avoid Girlfriend, Daveed unexpectedly bumps into Boss, as he, too, returns from the ladies restroom, also tracking cherry-red footprints in his wake. He's so knackered, he can barely see straight. Daveed breathes a sigh of relief. He hasn't been recognized.

As he brushes past Boss, he hears an order: "Get my car," demands Boss, reeking of alcohol and Gitanes. He hands Daveed a coaster with his plate number HARB668 to assist him in ID'ing the vehicle. Daveed obliges, if only to momentarily leave the raucous bar. Daveed finds Boss's Mercedes and dispatches sleeping Driver to retrieve his precious cargo. Daveed follows Driver inside, but Boss's focus remains on Daveed. He stares deeply into his ebony eyes, as if they shared a secret. His countenance turns troubled, and he sobers for a second in deep thought.

He pulls out his wallet, slips Daveed $400 and passes him his business card.

"Call me… for a job," he says.

As the night wears on, drunk Tara, who's lost all concept of time, wonders what's taking Stan so long. The heart-stopping screech from the back of the bar answers her question. The Shun knife has precisely pierced deep into Stan's heart.

MONICA

Monica is broken.

Her sister, Angelica, secured her freedom from the immigration detention center, but Josefina remains in the void. Angelica and Geovany stayed in Texas, working with the ACLU to find the precious 3-year-old, and Angelica, an immigration lawyer, strongly encouraged Monica to leave and go north, to Daveed in Manhattan. She'd be safer there, and now that she's legal, it would aid Daveed's citizenship petition as well.

Monica has only known Daveed for three years and eight months. She was slightly aware of him prior, as was everyone in Escuintla; since childhood, he was a runner for the Mara Salvatrucha gang, where his family reigned, though he never moved up the ranks. Tino, his older brother and protector, saw to that. Daveed knew nothing else, just poverty and allegiance to family. Tino, an MS-13 enforcer, arranged the marriage between his friend Osmin's 16-year-old sister and his 30-year-old brother. Daveed was tall and handsome, and Monica was mesmerized by the MS-13 serpent tattoo crawling up his neck. Daveed believed the snake to be a guiding force leading his path, until becoming an evil reminder ruling, ruining his life. Marriage would bring peace to *la familia*. Yes, for a short time. However, fortunes change, and when despair meets desperation, the rules dissolve, and a new guard takes charge.

Eddy, Osmin and Tino were beheaded, sitting in Osmin's 1956 Ford Crown Victoria, *El Cohete Turquesa*, the Turquoise Rocket, now ravaged by MS-13 serpents spray-painted all over the well-polished deathtrap.

On their wedding night, Monica became pregnant and eight months later, Josefina was born. There was a sea-change in Daveed. He wanted to wipe his hands clean, longing for a better future for Josefina and Monica, outside of Guatemala. He has fallen deeply in love with Monica. She, however, is not fully sold on Daveed. She knows his past and wonders if a man could shed his skin. She was pleased when he showed up in Texas with *la serpiente* scaled from his neck.

The last place they tracked little Josefina was a facility in Taos, New Mexico. There were 1,096 children there at the time, and 408 of those children were returned home. The remaining 688 remain unaccounted for, spread around the country. Angelica investigated each location, and prayed Josefina wasn't farmed out to Bethany Christian Services, an adoption center financially tied to then-Education Secretary Betsy DeVos.

This morning, Monica finds Boss's business card while gathering David's uniforms collecting in the corner of their one-bedroom walkup in the Lower East Side.

"Daveed, do you need it?"

"Nah, toss it."

He hates Boss, the old bitch who loathingly passed him as if he were invisible each time he entered the building of the dead girl. Daveed was quiet, rarely interacting with the tenants for his brief tenure there. He knew their secrets from their coming and goings. Yeah, he has no need for the old guy's card, although his 400 bucks came in handy in funding Angelica's legal filings.

He's taking Monica to work today. It's her 19th birthday. For Daveed, it's just another night bussing tables at Viva.

Surprisingly, waiting for him at Viva's front door is Boss.

"Hey, did'ya lose my card?" he asks.

Daveed wonders if Boss remembers him as Doorman. He pretends he's never seen him before.

"Your card? I think you have the wrong guy."

He's one handsome sonofabitch, Boss thinks. Daveed wouldn't be his first young man.

"I gave you my card and $400, a few weeks ago."

"Oh yeah. Thanks for that. Card must be lost. It was a hectic night."

Boss eyes the tattoo scar. This is definitely the guy.

"How'd you like a job? Be my driver. Would 2K a week work?"

Monica tugs Daveed's arm. Opportunities like this don't happen to people like them.

Wondering what Boss was really up to, he responds, "We never saw each other in our lives, why are you offering me this job?"

Boss wants to believe him, but can't take the chance, "Because you were kind and helpful to me that night."

Monica yelps, "Yes. Yes, he'll be happy to take the job, Mister."

BERDE

It's Berde's 87th birthday, but no one's around to celebrate now that Lallie's gone.

Lallie would always make a cake (not a very good one), and she'd invite Bill from 689, the LaRosas from 686, some nameless woman and her various girlfriends depending on the year from 682, and Old Theresa from 690. Old Theresa would bring her dachshund Marcellus. He,
Admiral Jackson and Sheldon would play together, while the humans partook of cake. Young Theresa from 680 was never invited.

"She's a snotty kid who could learn to smile every once in a while," Berde complains.

"Not like Lallie," she continues, "she was a very sweet girl."

Berde further reminisces: "Tig from 680 used to be invited, but Lallie told me he started to stalk her and he frightened her, so she cut off contact with him. Something serious happened there, but Lallie never really shared more than, 'There was an incident.' It was the same time Lallie said she'd tripped and broke her arm, and Tig said he was all scratched up by a feral cat at the vet office where he was a tech. I'm not a snoop, but it sounded fishy. Now when I see Tig in the hall, we only greet each other with a nod."

Berde gets misty: "Every year for the past six years, Bill would take a photo of us and the cake, and frame it for me. I wonder where *he* is. I'm sad no one's around to remember."

Margot, Berde's daughter, calls her at noon every birthday, and the grandkids get on the phone yelling, "Hi, Oma," and it's sad when they hang up.

"Oh, my doctor's office leaves a message with a pre-recorded group singalong of "Happy
Birthday," from the staff.

"I miss Lallie and her visits," Berde says. "She certainly didn't deserve what happened. Who would? I always thought she was lonely. Only her father visited. Often. He had a key. Sheldon didn't like him. I'd hear him hiss whenever her father would arrive. Unfriendly guy. I think it was her father.

"I miss Sheldon. He was a very dear dog. He'd snuggle up to anyone, except Lallie's Dad. Oh, dear. Did I say, 'dog?' I meant "cat." My memory's going. I think my mind is going too. I hear noises next-door all the time. Banging, scraping and sometimes, I think voices. Just the last few days, I've been thinking I hear meowing. Can you imagine?

"Ah, an old lady's mind."

Berde falls asleep. Naptime.

That night she hears keys fumbling at Lallie's door. Berde puts *Molly & Me* on pause, and jumps up from her couch, with the energy of a teenager. She startles Admiral Jackson. She scoots to her door, cracking it a bit. She sees Matty Lynn entering apartment 688. Berde, curious about how the rental is going (She heard about poor Workman), makes a beeline for Lallie's, startling Matty Lynn, who's awkwardly attempting to enter the apartment, juggling shopping bags while keeping the door as slightly ajar as possible. Berde's no help.

"Hi Berde, how are you?"

"It's my Birthday. 87. Would you believe?"

"Wow, Berde, happy birthday." She's holding the door closed, but attempts to hug Berde, who takes advantage of it and opens the door wide. "Here let me help."

They're greeted by…

"A cat?" Berde shrieks.

"Uh, uh," fumbles Matty Lynn, collecting her thoughts, "I just adopted this cat [true], but my roommate is allergic [she has no roommate], so my boss said I can keep it in this empty apartment until I find a new home for her [not true at all. And Boss hates cats].

"Oh, she's so cute. What's her name?"

"We named her Arya."

Brow wrinkles. "We?"

"Oh, my roommate and I. [Biggest lie of all.]

"I have to run, Berde, but happy birthday."

"Thanks, dear. Nice to see you…and Arya."

Berde scurries back to *Molly & Me*.

Matty Lynn sits on the newly bought kitchen chair, and sighs.

"Well, that was fun, huh?"

The kitchen lights blink three times.

Matty Lynn takes out a salad from the fridge and settles in for her visit.

FUNERAL

Stan's funeral was a sad to-do.

Only 28, he was far too young to die. And murdered yet.

The service was packed. His large family (mom, dad, stepmom, stepdad, at least six sets of assorted grandparents and step-grandparents, four brothers, two sisters, and five step-siblings, and aunts, uncles, nephews, nieces, and 21 cousins—first cousins). Tara's family was large also, no need to list them all, other than maybe her twin sister, Kara, who dated Stan before Tara did. Stan had many friends from childhood, middle school, high school and college. He attended NYU, so many of his college friends were still based in the city. He worked several jobs before his current one at Technology ER, employed as an "emergency technician," where he was on call for late-night emergencies. Sort of a 911 for urgent electronic and tech catastrophes. He loved working at Technology ER, even though he only started about a year and nine months ago. Every one of those 688 days was a challenge. He felt like an electronics Dr. House.

His company's most important client, Harbinger Finance & Realty, became his sole steady work. He's saved their corporate ass often, and they were grateful, so they requested he'd be their regular technician. He also knew all their secrets, from illegal financial transactions to everyone's private emails, but part of the appeal of hiring Technology ER was that they had a stellar reputation for religiously obeying non-disclosure agreements. Stan didn't even share with Tara the privileged, private information he had access to, as salacious and shocking as some of it was.

But he kept a journal. A very secret, well-hidden journal.

The last job he worked for Harbinger was the night of Lallie's murder. The apartment building's security system had crashed. Intercom system down. Wi-fi was down. So, Stan was called around 8 p.m., while he was on another job and was able to arrive around 10 and had it up and working by 12:30 a.m.

Around midnight, lost in his work, Stan was startled by the clomping of Boss's gigantic, expensive shoes as he was leaving the building.

"Hey, Boss," he called from behind Doorman's podium. Boss looked understandably upset, distracted. Of course, he was, Stan surmises. His building was off-grid for hours and he'll probably be swamped by all the tenants tomorrow.

"Hello, Stan," Boss replied shakily, obviously anxious to get the hell out of there. "I've been checking up on things with... Super."

"Yeah, it's almost fixed. It seems like the...."

"Good job," Boss shouts out, thumbs up, and out he's rushed as Driver holds an umbrella over his head, as he's whisked off to his Mercedes.

It was Boss who suggested Stan and Tara consider Lallie's apartment. He offered them a good employee discount, but in reality, he wanted to have that apartment rented so Gerarra and his cronies, and the media, would stop hanging around. He was also dealing with a crippled Workman and a lawsuit he'll fight to the end, but one he knows he'll never win. Boss put his best employee on this—Matty Lynn.

Boss knew he had no secrets from Stan, so he wanted to keep him close. Like Daveed. Keep him happy. And quiet. He was shocked seeing how much Stan was drinking at Viva that rainy, raucous night—the night Stan was murdered. Yes, intoxicated Stan made Boss very concerned.

At the end of the service, Boss and Tarly take Tara aside.

"Don't worry about finances," Boss assures Tara. "I have your back. Stan was family." He trusted Stan, but things have suddenly become more complicated, and he was wondering if, perhaps, once-trusted Stan shared secrets with Tara.

Keep her happy.

Tony-looking as ever, Tarly, in a Chanel form-fitting black minidress, blonde hair in a high, tight ponytail, and those giant raindrop diamond studs, glistening as bright as Tara's tears, hugs Tara tightly. No young, new widow was going to outshine her. Especially one who Tarly believed might be the girl her husband was having an affair with. There's no other explanation, she felt, for her cheap, rotten spouse to be this kind.

Matty Lynn and Ghost agree. Matty Lynn will drop the double moniker for "ML." It's easier for Ghost to type two letters rather than 10.

ML comes by daily. She tells Boss no one wants the apartment, it's unrentable; actually, she hasn't shown it since she and Ghost made their connection. Her visits are so commonplace, even Berde's no longer curious.

Once inside the apartment, she and Ghost say their hellos (The sink turns on. Or rather, Ghost turns the sink on), and ML feeds Arya. Ghost is working on feeding Arya, but she can't open wet-food cans yet, only dry-food bags. It often spills all over the floor, and it's a mess, so it's ML's job now.

ML tells Ghost about her day, working for Boss. Ghost gets quiet when his name comes up. It's not until a few weeks later when their communication is more refined and Ghost feels more comfortable discussing it, that the subject of her affair with Boss is revealed. It had been going on for two years. She'd visit his penthouse in the Harbinger Building, and he would sometimes come to her apartment. *Ah, "the Dad" Berde mentioned.* He treated her poorly. Nothing like her actual Dad, a kind midwestern farmer. He died two years ago. The timing of the loss and gain is obvious to ML.

ML was shocked. Lallie seemed so timid. An affair with a married man? And a man married to such a powerful woman.

Boss made it clear to ML that he'd sleep with her at a moment's notice, but she declined. Many times. She took it as part of the job—turning down Boss's advances.

Ghost and ML never discuss the murder. It was made obvious from the first time they communicated on their laptops. ML would never bring it up. Ghost often discussed that rotten day, her work problems that afternoon, the beet salad left uneaten, the relentless rain, the elevator ride with Bill, but once she entered 688 that evening—nothing. ML began to think Ghost had no idea who killed her.

Today, ML is a little moody, and it isn't triggered by the dark clouds and constant showers. She has to tell Ghost that she needs to rent out the apartment.

"Arrrrrrr," Ghost groans loudly. Berde perks up her ears. The wind?

Arya scampers into the bathroom, anticipating an unhappy conversation about to unfurl. ML turns off the TV she recently brought to watch *Big Bang Theory, Game of Thrones* and binge on *Star Trek* reruns with Ghost. Even in death Lallie remains a nerd.

"I'm being pressured," ML explains. "Boss."

Ghost groans again, "Arrrrrrr." Berde raises the volume on *Murder She Wrote,* amplifying Jessica Fletcher's warbly, prying voice into 688.

We'll figure something out. Maybe you'll learn to transport yourself by then.

"Yeah," Ghost types out, "Beam me up, Scotty."

They laugh. "Who knows," says ML.

Ghost types: "Want 2 go 2 Disneyworld."

"Sounds good to me. You'll certainly save us airfare," responds ML.

"Seriously. Want 2 go 2 Disneyworld. But I have some unfinished business 2 attend 2
first.

"Uhm, OK, that sounds a little ominous."

"It's dead serious."

"Well, when you're ready you can tell me about it."

Ghost types "Deal," then continues: "I've been thinking. I know where Boss keeps a lot of cash in the office. "

"Yeah, and...oh. Whoa. How are you gonna pull that off?"

"No, *you're* gonna pull it off," Ghost types. "If we have 2 move out of here, we need some $$$$."

ML is silent. It sounds like a plan. Boss deserves this.

"ML," Ghost types. "What if I can't leave here?"

"Let's get to that when the time comes," ML responds. "Just behave yourself when I bring prospective renters in."

"Will do."

They're interrupted by a loud commotion outside their window. Some guy just robbed an old man and he's running down the street away from the angry mob attending to the victim. Ghost watches intently. A cab, medallion 688, comes out of nowhere, skids on the rain-slicked street and strikes the mugger.

Maybe I *can* get to Disneyworld, Ghost wonders to herself.

AGENT

Phones buzzing throughout the office.

Most of the girls are fully booked, and TV, commercial and movie offers still pour in. Agent's assistant needs an assistant.

Girlfriend needs help, she fears. She's seen this meltdown before. Even in high school, she saw Girlfriend's erratic side. When Girlfriend was in medical school in Houston, Agent constantly encouraged her to switch careers, move to Manhattan and sign with her modeling agency. Girlfriend wouldn't hear of it. She was in love with her surgery professor and was well on her way to Doctordom. A surgeon had saved her mother's life when all odds were against her, and Girlfriend became obsessed. Now, with Professor in the picture, Agent realized that modeling was only her own dream for Girlfriend. Shame, Agent always thought, she's too beautiful for medicine.

However, Girlfriend finally came around. It took a bloody altercation with Professor; she with a black eye, he skillfully slashed by a scalpel. He taught her well. Professor, afraid of Girlfriend's rage and cutting skills, demurred on pressing charges on the one caveat that she'd leave town. And what career pays more than surgery? Modeling. By a lot. It was a no-brainer. Agent was thrilled to have her, and Girlfriend's career blew up from the start.

Girlfriend was fortunate. Agent teamed her with a talented young photographer, Bill. It was attraction at first sight. Why not? Girlfriend was gorgeous, and Bill's camera adored her. Intertwined, they both quickly rose to the top of their fields. Agent, like Girlfriend's mother, couldn't understand the couple's allure for each other. Girlfriend had handsome male superstars in many fields— sports, modeling, acting, music, business—smitten with her. When Girlfriend focuses, she remains focused as if staring through a rifle's sight; her vision fixed on Bill from Day One. Bill had his share of groupies too. His world was constantly filled with beautiful, sexy models, all at his command. "Lean to the left!" "Hand in hair!" "Slump in the chair!" "Pout!" "Jump!" "Expose your left breast."

Agent is worried about Girlfriend. She hasn't returned her calls. This is how she was after Professor, so it concerns Agent deeply. She knows the depths Girlfriend can sink.

She dials the phone.

"Bill? Where the hell are you? I'm worried that you're not returning my calls. My star model is incommunicado and now my star photographer has gone silent. If I don't hear from you by tonight, I'm coming over and beating the crap out of you. I'm worried about you both. Did you have some sort of fight? Are you secreted away with her in Fiji? Are you on a shoot for another agency? Call me, you crazy bastard."

On Bill's end, the call just goes into the clutter of other inbox messages from his mom, his siblings, assorted magazines, Bella Hadid, Berde and a number of curious anonymous hang-ups.

The thought crosses Agent's mind: I hope she hasn't hurt him.

She shakes it off. Agent hopes Bill might have just freaked from his neighbor being slaughtered and is getting some R&R. That, though, is unlike him, although what is like him has changed recently. He's turned inward; become antisocial. He's been acting secretive and, to be honest, a bit shady. She had asked Girlfriend about it, but she laughed it off.

"He's just super busy," Girlfriend responded. But later that night she called Agent, depressed about Bill's current behavior.

Girlfriend's about to lose a big payday. *Vogue Italia* has a cover feature for her, for a new perfume, Rain, by Givenchy. Two weeks in Rome. Valentino supplying the clothes. Top stylist Jessica Pater would do her magic. Beyoncé's set designer was working on a shimmering rainstorm. Agent has 43 boxes, each containing 16 bottles of Rain, she needs to get to Publicist to deliver to 688 fashion and style writers around the world.

But best for Agent: A large check from *Vogue*, and an even larger one from Givenchy.

Agent loves those meaty checks. But she only has one more day to make this happen, and Girlfriend is hiding away somewhere. Shame, Agent thinks, Girlfriend looks so beautiful in the rain.

SANDRA

"It's as easy as pie," Ghost says. She's progressed to text-to-speech.

"Maybe for you. I've never stolen from anyone before," ML's adamant. "I've never done anything illegal."

"It's not really stealing, if you're taking money from a crook."

"I don't know."

"ML, Boss exploited you, me and 99 percent of his workers and clients. He has more money than he knows what to do with, and he probably wouldn't even notice it was missing, if it weren't for…"

"The empty safe?"

They laugh at the absurdity of their situation.

"You really hate him?" ML asks.

"To the core. He used me. Treated me like garbage. He might have even killed me."

It's the first time Ghost even broached the subject.

"You don't know who killed you?"

"No. It was traumatic, you know."

"That's an understatement," ML jokes.

"Seriously, I can't remember anything about that night."

"Maybe you were roofied."

"Well, Gerarra'll figure it out. I know who, I'm sure. I just can't conjure it up."

"Look, a few weeks ago, you barely communicated through a water faucet. Now you're talking electronically and texting (ML got her a cell). You'll get there." ML was always so reassuring.

"Let's recap," Ghost suggests. "The safe's in Sandra's office. Make an appointment with her. Tomorrow's Toddy's birthday. They're all leaving early for *Wicked*. Ugh, I wish I was with them. Toddy's so fun and I'm dying to see that show." Ghost refocuses. "She'll be the last one there. When you leave her, just hide in ladies room. I don't think she ever pees. Oh, I wish I was doing this."

"Why didn't you do this before?" ML queries her invisible friend.

"Something's changed."

"Duh," ML, the change, snorts.

"The safe's behind the Monet print. As Boss's personal assistant *and girlfriend*, I set up the keypad combination. It's my apartment number 688: We were the only two who knew it. Think about it…since I'm dead, who's he gonna blame? The perfect crime. Oh, I wish I could be there with you."

****

In Sandra's tidy, spacious office, I'm reminded that she's a talker. And a crier. And a gossip. She's trying my patience.

She greets me with a perky, "So nice to see you, Matty Lynn. Sorry, I have to rush you.

It's Toddy's birthday today. We're going to *Wicked*." She whispers, "Toddy's gay."

I know.

"If Boss found out, he'd fire him," Sandra says conspiratorially. Blah. Blah. Blah. "So, you can't rent out Lallie's?"

"No," I answer, politely

"Lallie was sweet," says Sandra wistfully. Waterworks, like when she was on the news.

"So sweet."

"Yes, she is."

"Was," Sandra, corrects me.

"Yes, was."

I extend my hand. "Sandra thanks for everything." It's been 45 minutes of blah, blah, blah.

Sandra waves off the handshake and hugs me goodbye. "Anytime, hon."

I walk through the empty office and slam the main door shut hoping Sandra believes I've left. I sneak into the ladies room, in the back stall, quiet as can be. I listen as Sandra's high heels clickety-clack their way through the office to the door and then jangling of keys. I peer out the bathroom door and hear the clickety-clack diminish down the hallway to the elevator.

I race into Sandra's office and approach Monet's "Women in a Garden," put on gloves, pull at the frame, extend it from the wall, and *voila*, in front of my eyes is the safe's keyboard.

I punch in 6-8-8. It's open. I speedily scoop the cash into my bag, heart accelerating with every move. Filled with adrenaline, I slam the safe closed, throw my gloves in my handbag with all the green, and hightail it back to the apartment. *Easy peasy*, Ghost thinks to herself.

ML's hyped-up like a junkie. She's officially a thief. A robber. A criminal. And she loves it. Ghost loves it even more. Her crimes, however, seem more sinister. In both cases, they are now addicted to danger.

****

ML pours the money on the couch. Over the next hour, they count and recount: $2.4 million.

The dirty money now in the hands of two more deserving, a girl and her ghost.

YOLANDE

Boss and Tarly are in foul moods.

He, because he's always foul and he's dreading tonight's banquet in his honor. She, because everything Boss-related irks her. But worse, her night to be in the spotlight is up against the damn Met Gala, attended by Everyone Who Is Anyone. Boss's banquet will now include Everyone Who's Leftover.

Honor aside, neither Boss nor Tarly are self-made successes: Boss's parents' multimillion-dollar inheritance. Tarly's skilled surgeons and Boss's wealth. She wasn't his first choice. That was Brenda from Buffalo who Boss married at 22. Tarly worked hard to get Boss.

Boss walks to the bar, pours a scotch; deep amber ripples from the drop of two ice cubes. Yolande enters the room excitedly exclaiming, "Thank you very much for your generous gift for my brother's wedding." Boss doesn't respond. Doesn't need to, Tarly's making her grand entrance. An Ice Queen, maybe, but she's a formidable beauty in her royal-red Versace gown, perfectly sculpted and painted face, blonde hair in a high, tight ponytail, the bottom of which lightly flutters on her glistening bare shoulders. The giant raindrop diamonds glittering on her ears.

Yolande sighs, placing her hand over her heart. "Oh, Ma'am. You're *muy bonita*."

"English here, Yolande," Tarly, who just wants it repeated, scolds. "Have you seen my sapphire necklace? The Harry Winston?"

"It's in the Lavender Suite, Ma'am, just where you told…"

Tarly's already gone. Upstairs in the Lavender Suite, she mists her neck with Roja Haute Lux Parfum from its $3,500 3.4-ounce crystal dispenser. Returning downstairs, she has orders for Yolande.

"Make sure Driver picks up Britt after her riding lesson at 7. Dallas' mom will be here at 6:30 to bring Chase to the Mother-Son Dance. They'll need dinner. Madison and Maddison have a sleepover tonight. When Maddison arrives, make sure she washes her hands."

The bell rings and Yolande lets Daveed in. No one says goodbye to Chase or Madison, but Squiggles gets a few kisses from Tarly. Daveed holds an umbrella over Tarly as he walks her to the car, shielding her from the powerful squalls. He then does the same with Boss.

Fortunately, Daveed has a chauffeur's cap, so at least his head is dry.

*****

Sandra's wary about hiring the only event planner left available this day. Most details are left to him, but Sandra's in charge of the tribute film.

During cocktails, Tarly makes the rounds. She's good at this, and people feel more affluent just being in her presence. The Man of Honor sits at his table, grudgingly accepting well-wishers. The lights dim for the film presentation and when Tarly arrives at the table she's enraged. Furious. Sitting next to Boss is new-widow Tara. Tarly bares her bright veneers in a vicious smile and tightly hugs the girl she believes is her husband's new mistress.

Sandra's sweating bullets as the event gets into gear. Lights dim, and her featurette, directed by Toddy, Harbinger's in-house videographer, and his boyfriend, Len, flickers on large screens around the room.

Boss and Tarly are horrified. They've spent a lifetime keeping their secrets, and here they're on display for the world to see.

Daveed settles in a corner table. Boss told him to stay so he'd be ready to ferry him off at a moment's notice.

Buffalo. A dreary place for this upscale crowd. Rough and tumble Boss and Tarly as children. Boss's parents' butcher shop, Buffalo Butchery, thriving, always competing against Tarly's parents' butcher shop. (Toddy received this rare footage from Boss's older, estranged brother.) Boss apprenticing at 12 and two years later becoming such a prodigy, he's earned the title Master Butcher. His nickname: The "Cut-'Em-Up Kid." Boss's parents' millions set him up at Harbinger at 22. Tarly mirrored Boss's butchery expertise, but as a girl, no one cared. An embarrassing secret. Maybe it's good the A-list is strutting at the Met. Boss texts Sandra and Toddy: Ur fired.

Fuming. Boss feels exposed, but the guests are enthralled, clicking their wine glasses, chanting "Cut-'Em-Up Kid."

Det. Gerarra, too, stands at full attention, furiously notetaking.

Meanwhile, Yolande is in the Lavender Suite trying on Tarly's rust-red wig.

TODDY

ML's at her desk, lost in thought, twiddling her pen through her fingers, when she's startled by Receptionist: "Toddy's on the phone."

Without hesitation, "Please put him through."

"Hello, Toddy," she says, a bit guiltily. She feels bad she hadn't called him since his firing at the Banquet fiasco. She hasn't had the time. Feeling under the weather, she's exhausted running between work and her secret life with Ghost. "So good to hear from you."

Tearful Toddy dramatically whispers, "I need your help, Matty Lynn."

"Oh, no, Toddy, what's wrong?"

"It's Len."

"Oh, God, is he OK?"

"We've broken up." Could this day get any bleaker? Business is slow, her energy level's depleted, the torrent outdoors, and now Toddy's sad news. He and Len have been together for forever.

"Toddy, I'm so sorry to hear this." ML wonders why he's calling to share this news.

"I need a place to stay. Like today. I'm downstairs with all my things." (In Harbingerspeak, "downstairs" usually means Viva.) He pauses as he tries to contain his sobs. "Can I stay at Lallie's?"

"Uhm, well…" think fast, ML, "the truth is, Toddy, I've been fighting with my roommate (that fake roommate, again) so I've been staying there."

Toddy wails, "Oh, please, Matty Lynn, he beat me. I'm hurt. Please."

ML's heart is breaking for him. "OK, Toddy, I'll be right down."

****

Berde is walking down the hall with Admiral Jackson as ML and Toddy exit the elevator weighed down by Toddy's possessions. ML is carrying his giant stuffed bear, which frightens Admiral Jackson.

"It's OK," Berde assures him. "It's only a toy."

As soon as they get into the apartment, ML rapidly repeats the history of what's going on, so Ghost knows not make her presence known.

"SoToddyI'msosorryyouandLenbrokeupbutI'mgladyoucanstayher
euntilyougetsettled."

"You're a godsend, Love."

ML turns off the computer and sits down on the couch.

Toddy looks around, "Aww, I miss Lallie. She was always so
sweet."

The lights flash.

ML, looking exasperated, "There's a short."

Ghost notices Toddy has a black eye, a split lip, a broken index
finger, and his arms are bruised.

"She's Arya," ML offers, as the cat rubs against Toddy, quickly
succumbing to his petting, already BFFs.

"That's so cool," Toddy purrs. Ghost notices scratches on
Toddy's neck. She thinks of Tig.

"Gotta go, Toddy," ML says. "Have a good night's sleep. We'll
talk tomorrow."

"Bye, all," she shouts.

Her phone vibrates. "Poor Toddy," Ghost texts.

"Behave!" ML responds.

Ghost sends the laughing/crying emoji.

ML shakes her head, and leaves.

Toddy curls up with Stefon, his giant Teddy, and falls asleep on
the floor. Ghost watches over him. She brushes her hand against his
head several times while he's sleeping.

At 2 a.m., both Toddy and Ghost are rattled by *Wicked*'s
"Defying Gravity," Toddy's ringtone. It's contrite, tearful Len,
effusively apologizing.

"OK," Toddy compromises, "I'll text where I am, but no
promises." Ghost wants to scream "No Toddy!" but ML's earlier
text requesting she behave takes precedence.

Toddy primps for the 35-minute wait for Len. He shares the
elevator in silence with Tig, hood up, looking ominous. Toddy waits
in the lobby for Len as Tig walks into the humid, rainy night. Tig
bumps into Len as they enter/exit and they both snarl and move on.

Upstairs in the apartment, Len couldn't be more affectionate. But
Toddy's not buying it; bravely standing his ground. Ghost wishes
she had popcorn. Len apologizes profusely, but Toddy brings up past
abusive incidents.

"I don't love you anymore," Toddy says sadly.

That's when Len stands up and sucker punches Toddy out cold. Ghost scans Toddy's bruised, battered and broken body.

In the kitchen, Len rips Stefon from head to toe, sprinkling stuffing all over Toddy, like a gentle snowfall. He leaves. He continues pressing the elevator button but no-go. He takes the stairs. There's a whimper, bang and tumble, tumble, tumble, as Len bounces from step to step. He's bruised. He stands and slips again, falling hard on the landing. He's battered. Losing consciousness, he leans over the banister. Losing balance, he falls down the stairwell. He's broken.

Ghost is getting stronger.

"Man, I'm thirsty," ML says, downing about a quart of water. "I also have interest in the apartment. I'm showing it on Wednesday."

"I'll get my sheet ready," jokes Ghost.

"No, I'm serious, I have to rent it out. Boss is getting suspicious."

"Ugh. They better not be creeps."

"I'll write in a no-creeps clause."

"What about Toddy?"

"I love him to pieces," says ML, "but he's really a strain being here, with you hiding and me sneaking visits. This could be a blessing in disguise."

"Well, at least we have two days while he's visiting his sister."

"I'm going to tell him my roommate moved out and I'll let him move in with me for the time being. He's a lot of fun. I don't mind him around."

"Hey, I certainly love him. I'm number one on his mind, with this documentary he's doing about my murder. He just needs to stay safe."

"Well if this documentary has one tenth of the impact of his film at Boss's tribute, it ought to be killer. Oops, sorry."

They both laugh.

"Let's clean up. We're getting company."

****

On Wednesday, when ML arrives, she looks ill. Bags under her eyes, dry flakey skin. The constant rain isn't helping her health, and she needs to turn these trips around the city into actual productive exercises. She's carrying a large water bottle and paperwork she just picked up from her urgent care center with blood results from tests she took last week. She looks and feels awful.

ML is accompanied by a perky young woman, Dr. Tate Senders, a 28-year-old resident at NYU Medical Center who looks like she could be Mayim Bialik's twin. She's accompanied by her parents. This is her first apartment on her own, and it's just her and her cat, Weasley. Ghost likes her right away.

ML explains that a friend is staying there temporarily, and he'll be out by tomorrow and the apartment will be cleaned. She then provides Harbinger's standard murder disclaimer, but they already know all about it, and take a very pragmatic approach. It doesn't bother them. New Yorkers. Doctor is ready to move in on the first of the month, a week from today. They make arrangements to meet at Harbinger to sign the papers tomorrow. This new arrangement will satisfy Boss, but it will certainly upend ML and Ghost's world. They'll figure it out.

As Doctor leaves the apartment, she spots ML's blood test results on the kitchen counter. She catches herself as she looks it over and apologizes profusely.

"No, No. That's fine. What do you think?" ML asks.

"I think you have Type 2 Diabetes. May I?" She points to the computer on the counter.

ML scurries to close conversations she was having with Ghost.

Doctor pulls up the Mayo Clinic page for Diabetic Hyperosmolar Syndrome.

"Your blood sugar level is 688, a strong indication of this syndrome. This can be a serious condition, so you need to stay ahead of it. What are your symptoms?"

"I've been extremely exhausted. I'm super thirsty… "

Observing ML's face, "I see dry mouth and skin."

"Yeah, totally, and occasional fevers."

"Seems like it. You need to see your GP, or you can come to me. You need meds. Meanwhile, watch your diet and get exercise."

ML's text buzzes: "Ask her if it's forever."

"Is this a chronic condition?"

"No, not necessarily, but it can be fatal if untreated." She hands ML her card, "We'll go over everything."

"I'll call your office for an appointment tomorrow."

"Ask her how you got it," Ghost texts.

"How did I get it?"

"An infection? Some illness? Even diuretics."

The lights flash.

"Oh, just a short that we're taking care of this afternoon."

Ghost warned ML about the water pills she'd been taking to be able to fit in that slinky dress for the Banquet.

They say their goodbyes, and Doctor says, "I really like the vibe here." Ghost smiles.

After they leave, ML whispers, "I told you I was feeling sick!"

In the elevator, with Tig, Doctor's parents share concerned glances.

Doctor thinks, *Hmm, he's cute*.

TIG

Tig has kept his eye on Lallie's apartment.

He dawdles a bit by her door, pretending he's adjusting his headphones or tying his sneaker. Sometimes he hears meowing, and other times muffled voices, one which sounds robotic; must be the TV he saw ML bring the other day.

Lately his eye's on Doctor.

Today, he sits in the interrogation room, waiting to be interviewed. Enter Detectives Gerarra and Hammerstein. Now all Tig needs to do is figure out who's good cop and who's bad.

"Tigson, thanks for coming down," Gerarra starts. He doesn't look like a cop. He looks like a tussle-haired philosophy professor.

"It's Tig," he says, removing his hood. He's goateed, gaunt and intense looking, and surprisingly composed.

"He's a pro at this," Gerarra thinks to himself.

"OK, Tig, thanks for coming down." Ah, Gerarra's good cop. Watch out for him.

"Did I have a choice?"

"Sure, and we appreciate it, Tig," Gerarra responds. "Positive you don't want a drink? A lawyer?" Hammerstein glares. He looks like a cop.

"Yes." Tig waits for the questions.

"You knew Lallie, correct?

"Yep."

"Did you see her the night of her murder?"

Tig takes a second to think of how to answer. "Yes."

"What time?"

"Around 6:30. She just came home from work. She was with Bill. They always take the elevator up together around dinnertime."

Gerarra and Hammerstein scribble notes.

"See her again?"

"Yes. Around 10. Internet was out so I went to Dunphy's for a drink. I was walking down the hall, and I saw her closing her door. She'd just let someone in."

"Did you see who?

"No."

"Male or female?"

"I didn't see."

"What time did you get back?

"One."

"Anyone see you?"

"No, Doorman was gone."

"Anyone see you at the bar?"

"Yeah, I guess. Bartender. Whoever was there."

"Bartender will vouch for you being there three hours?" Hammerstein pipes in.

"I guess."

"You a regular there?"

"Nah. Never been there before."

"Why'd you choose Dunphy's?"

"It's the closest to the apartment. I was tired. But it's kind of a dump. Not my scene."

"If it wasn't your scene, why'd you stay there so long?"

"I was tired. Lazy."

"Tig, think carefully. Did you see anything strange when you returned?"

"Just a spinning hallway. Actually, I smelled something. The hallway between 689 and Lallie's smelled of curry. I hate curry."

"Anything else?"

Tig thinks, "Her door might have been open a smidge."

"An inch, two inches, a foot?

"No. More like a quarter inch."

"Did you look inside?"

"Nah, Berde opened her door so I wanted to avoid that scene."

Hammerstein throws two thick, juicy files on the table.

"How well did you know Lallie?"

"We went out for a while."

"How long?"

"Long enough."

Gerarra asks, as good cop. "What went wrong, Tig?"

Tig looks up at Gerarra, smirks, and for the first time makes eye contact. "She was a psycho?"

"A psycho? What do you mean?"

"She'd be sweet as anything one day, and the next she'd be paranoid, violent. And psycho."

The two cops look at each other.

"You a shrink?" Hammerstein taunts.

Eye contact again. "As a matter of fact, I am, officer. I have a PhD in psychiatry." Silence. Silence.

"So, you think she was mentally unstable?"

"Yes. Paranoid and psychotic."

"How was she paranoid?"

"She accused me of stalking her."

"Were you, Tig?"

"We were dating."

"How was she psychotic?"

"There were times when she was devoid of empathy, compassion. You want my full diagnosis? Pay me as a consultant."

"And violent? How was she violent?"

"She instigated physical altercations. I defended myself, but she instigated. She would injure herself and say, 'Look what you did.'"

"Did you do those things?"

"Not those things."

Hammerstein pats the two fat files. "You know what this is?"

"I can imagine."

"Complaints and trial transcripts from two other women saying you were violent,"

Hammerstein taunts. "It's 688 pages of nasty stuff about you."

"Was I in prison?"

"What do you mean?"

"Just what I asked, was I in prison? I don't think so. Time's up fellas. Next time call my lawyer."

REDHEAD

There have been many film projects Toddy's been involved with in his videography career, but none have been as meaningful as *688*, his documentary about Lallie's death.

He and Lallie were work friends who enjoyed sharing drinks at Viva, meeting for an occasional movie, or sharing pizza while watching DVR'd *RuPaul's Drag Race* on Sundays after a midday brunch. He always liked her, but he was never as obsessed with her as he's become after her death. Especially when he was staying in her apartment, with her presence palpable all around him, as if she were there.

He's at Berde's today to film her, and she's in the bathroom "putting on [her] face" while he sets up the camera and has Admiral Jackson sniffing at his feet. Berde, finally all gussied up, sits on the couch powdered, painted, and patting her butterscotch hair making sure it's set properly for her movie debut. Admiral Jackson's now sitting on the pillow on the chair by the window, hypnotized by the rain pelting the glass.

"Tell me something, Berde, about Lallie that we might not already know. Something about that night."

"I think I know Lallie's secret. She's…" There's a loud crash in the hallway. They both rush to the door as Admiral Jackson sounds the alarm. Bark. Bark. Bark.

In the hallway, there are split-open boxes and assorted bathroom items splayed all over the floor. Crest whitening toothpaste. ZeroXeno Lemongrass Kombucha shampoo. Sundries like that. And six rolls of Charmin Ultra Soft.

"Oh, so sorry," says Doctor apologizing to everyone standing around. Little Theresa looks outside her door, down the hall, and then slams the door shut. Toddy bends down to help Doctor and Tig pick up the mess that was strewn when Doctor, blinded by the boxes she was carrying in front of her, slammed into Tig, on his way to the elevator, deeply engrossed in an article, "The Rise of the Creative Class," on *The New York Times'* Twitter feed. Or maybe he did see her.

After everything is picked up and helped carried into her new apartment, introductions. When Tig extends his hand to shake

Doctor's hand, the environmentally friendly ZeroXeno glass bottle that he picked up in the hallway suddenly cracks open and he's covered in lemongrass shampoo. Ghost is not happy.

"Oh, let me help you with that," Doctor says, leading him to the kitchen, and wiping his clothes with her dish towel. Ghost doesn't like the direction this is taking. Tig, on the other hand, is liking it a lot. He looks around the apartment. It feels weird.

Toddy interrupts. "Hi, Tig, happy to meet you. I'm working on a documentary about Lallie, and I'm actually in the midst of interviewing Berde now, would you mind sitting for an interview?" Berde has brought Admiral Jackson back to her apartment after he began licking the shampoo off the floor.

Tig lives by first impressions, and he likes Toddy. "Sure, man. When?"

Toddy's a little more excited about this than he expected. He thought Tig was hot, but he's a sucker for that bad-boy hoodie look.

"Tomorrow around this time? I have Berde now, and tonight I'm interviewing Bill's Girlfriend. Did you know her?"

Tig hesitates. "Sorta."

Toddy's off to continue Berde's interview. "Nice to meet you all. I'll see you tomorrow, Tig."

Back in 687. "Berde, who do you think killed Lallie?"

"I know Little Theresa calls me a busybody, but I like to be aware of my surroundings. I've lived here for almost 60 years, so I'm very protective of it. I saw a lot going on that night. But first, what I was trying to tell you before…"

"Who did it, Berde?"

"Could be anyone. Tig…you'll see. Bill… he and Lallie, well, you know. The Girlfriend…jealous, obviously. Doorman. Dangerous-looking, and where'd he disappear to? The grouchy man who I'm now pretty sure was Lallie's boyfriend and not her father. And that redhead."

As Toddy enters his Uber, he realizes that Berde never finished telling him Lallie's secret when they were interrupted by the hallway crash. He'll catch her tomorrow when he films Tig.

SPUDS

Ghost thinks it's time that she introduces herself to Doctor.

She likes her a lot. Why not? She's funny and lonely and is dedicated to Arya, gifted to her by ML. And Weasley's cool. Ghost adores Doctor's taste in TV (*Fleabag, Doctor Who*, and of course, even lay-people's favorite medical show, *Grey's Anatomy*) and she appreciates that they have the same taste in men (Tig), although Ghost isn't completely thrilled that Doctor and Tig have been dating for the last month, since Doctor moved in.

 It's been tough not seeing ML that often. ML's been so ill, she had to take leave from work. Now her medical team is wondering if it might be cancer and not just diabetes. The timing of Toddy moving in with ML when Doctor rented apartment 688 turned out to be perfect. Besides being the ideal roommate (his rent is always on time, thanks to a grant he received for the documentary, which he quietly, slavishly edits in his bedroom when he's not out filming interviews), he has also become ML's extremely grateful, dedicated and honored nursemaid. Doctor has taken over ML's medical care, and ML's friends and family all believe she's been a literal lifesaver.

Ghost is afraid that ML will die. So is Toddy. So is ML. Ghost thinks that if she makes friends with Doctor, she, too, can become an influence in ML's healthcare decisions.

Doctor and Ghost have been living together for a month, and Ghost has been very well behaved. It was her written promise to ML, via text. ML doesn't have to know that the fire in the deli across the street was payback for a previous minor insult when Lallie was alive. Or Mr. LaRosa's heart attack was payback for the time he attempted to put his hand up her skirt at one of Berde's birthday parties. Ghost thinks it was the 82nd. Or Little Theresa's cat, King Kong, getting loose one day, and the sixth-floor hallway window just happened to be open a crack large enough for a cat to squeeze through. Tig? He's being Groundhog Day'd. Seems he keeps "losing" his cellphone. Every day. He's been buying a new one each day for past two weeks so far. Ghost is waiting to see when he reaches both his emotional and financial limits and goes phoneless just out of frustration. He thinks he's going out of his mind.

No, Ghost is getting *into* his mind.

Doctor has a dentist appointment at 2; just for a cleaning. It is miserable out, and the streets are flooding from the forewarned Nor'easter, so she decides not to go back to work. Today is paperwork day, anyway. No appointments. She arrives home at 4 and decides she'd whip up an early dinner: salad, some leftover chicken, string beans, and a stuffed baked potato that she picks up on the way home from the niche bistro, Spuds, across the street. It looks so welcoming, Ghost thinks, wishfully eyeing all the customers entering and exiting.

Tig has some sort of 12-step "Anonymous" meeting tonight (he attends so many different ones, it's difficult keeping track of his schedule), otherwise it might be dinner for two, perhaps.

As jealous as she is, Ghost doesn't mind when he comes over; she misses him at times. When Doctor and Tig have sex, Ghost just hides in the guest bedroom.

Now that she has Doctor alone to herself tonight, Ghost thinks she'll take a chance.

She moves Doctor's plate. Doctor stops chewing and stares at the dish for a few seconds.

She checks the table, shakes her head, and resumes eating.

Ghost flashes the kitchen light three times. Doctor stands up, walks over to the light, stands on a chair to check the bulb, hand to chin, wonders for a second, steps off the chair and returns to her potato.

The faucet runs. Doctor throws down her fork, annoyed, marches to the sink, turns off the faucet, and stands with hands on hips. She surveys the room, walks over to her couch, sits, and just stares.

She looks up and asks meekly, in a whisper, "Lallie?"

Toddy introduces himself at the main gate as a filmmaker, and, fortunately, the guard is starstruck.

He lets Toddy's rented car right into Oak Estates, and Toddy drives through to Diamond Circle, Boss's house. With no cars in the expansive circular driveway, he second guesses whether he should have called first, but rings the front bell anyway. Yolande answers the door.

"Hi. I'm Toddy," he announces, fiddling with his heavy equipment case. I'm filming a documentary that includes Harbinger and I was hoping to interview…," he looks at her in her old-fashioned maid's outfit…, "your Boss."

"He's not in," Yolande says, not quite interested in ridding herself of this unsolicited visitor so fast. She waves him in, "Come in out of the rain."

"Thanks," says Toddy, entering the opulent foyer. Yolande takes his umbrella and raincoat.

"Boss won't be back until late," she tells Toddy. "I'm Yolande, their maid."

"How long have you worked here, Yolande?" Toddy asks, as she ushers him into the kitchen, where he sits down at the massive glass table. She sits next to him. The kitchen is spotless. Two adults, four children (Maddison was over again last night) all cleaned up after.

Yolande's new sister-n-law, Be'Linda, has babysitting duty for Yolande's own four kids today.

"Twelve years," she says, carefully containing the bitterness that has grown over her tenure here.

"Wow, you must know everything there is to know about the two of them," Toddy says, hopefully.

"Oh, Yes. Definitely, yes." He notices a flicker of fire in her eye. A documentarian's radar.

"Did you know Lallie? The girl who was killed?"

"She was Boss's friend."

Yolande was looking eager and Toddy was on a tight schedule. No need to dally.

"What was their relationship like?" he asks, jumping right into it.

Yolande had given her notice the day before. Tarly hardly reacted except for the moment she realized it would be an inconvenience finding someone new. Boss couldn't have cared less. Yolande will miss Squiggles, but she'll miss Britt most; she was a kind 17-year-old, an anomaly in this family. Yolande had nothing to lose now by being honest. She was such an insignificance to them, no one noticed that her non-disclosure agreement ran out two years ago.

"She was his girlfriend," she answers, with a vindictive smirk.

Toddy's taken aback. He arrived here expecting a frosty reception from Boss and Tarly, never expecting to hit the bullseye with their disgruntled maid.

"Can I film this interview?" Toddy asks.

Yolande brushes some errant hair from the side of her face. "Yes, sir."

Toddy starts unpacking his equipment.

"Can I put on some makeup, Mr. Toddy?"

"Yeah, sure. Set-up'll take a few minutes," Toddy assures her. Yolande excuses herself. Toddy assembles a small spotlight, and checks Yolande's seat for light settings. When she returns, she looks pretty. She usually looks so haggard here at Boss's house.

"Is it good for the camera, Mr. Toddy?" she asks, pointing to herself.

"You look beautiful, Ms. Yolande," Toddy answers, paying her more respect in these minutes than she's received in this home for a dozen years. Yolande smiles broadly. She has a beautiful, warm smile.

Camera on, Toddy asks, "Yolande, please tell me about your Boss."

After a 5-minute non-stop litany of grievances, Toddy believes he has enough background. No holding back now.

"OK, Yolande. Let's talk about Lallie. What can you tell me about her relationship with Boss?"

Yolande discusses the affair, the key to Lallie's apartment she knew he had, and the impact Lallie's death had on the family, ("there was much tension that week"). She stops abruptly and says, "Mr. Toddy, I want to show you something." Camera still running, he follows her upstairs to the Lavender Suite, where Yolande walks up to a tacky, gold antique dresser, digs through some items, and pulls out a rust-red wig.

"It's Ms. Tarly's," she says with a wicked grin even broader than her earlier one. It's the wig she helped remove from distraught Tarly's rain-soaked head the night of the murder. Toddy reads the label: "Superstar Inc., 100% Human-hair Wigs. Style 688: The Rita Hayworth."

APOSTLE PAUL

In his cell, all Daveed has is a Bible.

He already knows it back and forth. Indoctrinated since he was a child in Guatemala. God was even by his side during the darkest of his MS-13-adjacent days, but God had fallen out of favor with him ever since Monica was detained and Josefina was kidnapped by ICE. Yes, he's rethinking the God thing now.

Daveed is reading "The Epistle of Paul the Apostle to The Ephesians," page 688 of the King James Bible. Paul wrote the letter to the Ephesians while he was imprisoned in Rome and unsure of his fate. Daveed can identify.

Rediscovering Paul's teachings, he finds he likes the message of God planning for Jesus to create a diverse community of believers and followers who live together as one, in unity, because of God's grace. Well, Daveed believes in that, too. He loves his God. He loves his church back home, and all the childhood innocence it conjures. He loves his family left behind, he loves his country of birth, he loves what America stands for, he even loves the feeling of camaraderie he had while observing his neighborhood gang, and he loves his wife and daughter. He needs to be a believer now. He, like Paul, has to know that though he might be imprisoned, his mind is free. He has to believe that some source of goodness, some higher power, will assist him in getting Josefina back, safe and sound.

Now, however, he's been worrying about being in jail, held for questioning. Of course, he's The Immigrant. The brown-skinned Outsider. A possible gang member, whose past was, in fact, grim. Observing robberies, murders, beheadings, like Lallie's. He's seen it all. The Doorman, who never smiled at the residents; he had more important things on his mind.

And the sudden disappearance.

Fact is, he was being driven to Texas that evening, no choice about it, and he wasn't one for goodbyes. His employers mistreated him. He asked them for an emergency leave of absence. He told them about Josefina. No response. That's why he left in the middle of the night, and why he has no alibi, except for his driver, who vaporized into air the minute he deposited Daveed in Laredo. All

Daveed can count on now is Monica, Angelica, Paul the Apostle, and Lawyer who Boss hired.

It's been months, and he and Boss still dance around each other, pretending they don't know each other from That Night. And Boss, who likes his enemies close, is panicked that Daveed's in jail and could easily blurt out secrets that need not be disseminated. Boss hired Lawyer to relieve Daveed of his current predicament or have him officially charged with Lallie's murder. Both options were convenient. The former would keep whatever Daveed knows about him secret, and the latter would divert attention from Boss, if it ever became known that he and Lallie were lovers and he was in her apartment the night of the murder. Oh, yeah, there's that "Cut-'Em-Up Kid" thing, too.

Fortunately, there's nothing solid to legally hold Daveed in jail for more than 96 hours without formal charges, so Lawyer secured Daveed's release, where chances of his snitching significantly lessened. Both men were tangoing, hoping they could trick the authorities into thinking the other was the prime suspect.

While Daveed was imprisoned, Monica furiously searched through his belongings that had been put in storage to find his Green Card documentation. The last thing they needed was for him to be deported. She searched the metal trunk, with double locks, which Monica had to hire a locksmith to remove for $200, because Daveed conveniently "forgot" where the key was. He must discourage this search. With her husband's freedom at stake, she was not the discouraged kind, so she had the locks removed. At the bottom of the trunk was the Green Card documentation and mementos of Daveed's hang-along gang days—three 9mm handguns, a clown mask and a butcher knife sharp enough to behead someone in one clean swipe.

Monica crosses herself, and moans "*Por que?*"
Solo Daveed sabe….
Y Dios."

MARCUS

It's a tough week for Ghost.

Doctor, Tig, Arya and Weasley are in the Bahamas, and ML's chemo is starting to take its toll on her. She hasn't been able to visit or text for weeks. Ghost is pissed. With everyone gone, she has lots of time to think. That's dangerous. There's just so much she can do to torture Little Theresa and anonymous passersby on the street.

She's angry at ML for abandoning her; she's been making up malicious stories about her to Doctor, who's shocked by ML's alleged out-of-character behavior. The verbal abuse Ghost describes to Doctor is bad enough, but she adds that she often wonders if ML might be her killer, for the fee she'd receive for renting the apartment. Yes, ML was that coldhearted and cruel, Ghost tells Doctor, her new BFF.

"Don't trust her," spurned Ghost said.

On Day 3 of Doctor and Tig's trip, bored with making up melodies to the patter of rain on the window and watching drenched crowds scoot in and out of Spuds, Ghost thinks about Marcus, her first boyfriend back home in Kansas. He was so handsome, and as an outlier, her brief romance with him brought her into a circle of friends, the likes of which she never encountered before. In fact, she never had any friends before. Not because she wasn't likable. She could be that. Or she was ugly. She certainly wasn't. Or she smelled or had ratty clothes. She was well taken care of. She just didn't care. She had no need for friends. Their petty interactions were meaningless to her. Their joys did not bring her joy, and their sorrows never moved her.

She was as emotionally flat as the bleak landscape outside her Midwest bedroom window.

Tessa wasn't really her friend. They hung out, had sleepovers, went to parties together, but Lallie never really connected with Tessa. With anyone. Maybe Lallie was prescient knowing it would be Tessa who'd steal Marcus from her.

Even though photos of Lallie's beaten body were banned by local media because she was only 17, somehow one made its way through social media. However, Marcus' mugshot was prominently circulated. Friends supported him at first, but when Lallie's photo made the rounds, all bets were off. He was ostracized, Tessa broke up with him, and Lallie was homeschooled, once again isolated from human contact of peers.

Today, on Day 3 of Doctor and Tig's trip, it was the first time Lallie thought about Marcus since the incident, and her subsequent move to New York City. She has never had a pang of guilt about uploading that photo of her bruised body, and never a second thought about beating the crap out of herself to make it seem she was beaten by good-hearted Marcus. They did have a physical altercation, starting with Lallie punching Marcus in the gut. Marcus, attempting to keep his distance from his suddenly crazed girlfriend, kept her at arms' length, and she tripped over Joey Tribbiani, her cat, and banged her head, scratching her face on the coffee table in the den.

"Get out. Get the fuck out," she yelled at him.

In a state of shock, seeing Lallie's sudden personality transform, Marcus ran home. That's when Lallie completed the beating. When her parents arrived home, they found their hysterical daughter, bruised, beaten and bloody. They called the police. On Day 3 of the Bahama trip, Lallie wonders if, after all these years, Marcus is out of prison yet. He probably wouldn't have liked Yale anyway.

Ghost doesn't know what she has in store for Tig. She has to determine what all the implications might be. Did she still have feelings for him? Would he love her again? Is he going to take up all of Tessa's, uhm, Doctor's time and attention? Would Doctor move away if Tig was gone, one way or another?

Meanwhile, she is pissed at ML, for being ill, not being here with her and letting these bad thoughts occupy her mind, or whatever it's called now.

"I'm done with her," Ghost says, closing that chapter without any regrets.

STUART

Bill's apartment has been uninhabited since the night of the murder.

His brother, Stuart, began paying the rent the past few months after realizing it was falling into arrears, so it would remain Bill's at his return. The family waited a week before they reported him as a Missing Person. They needed to check with Girlfriend and see if there was any photo shoot for which he was scheduled, which might have taken him out of town or out of the country for that matter. He had shoots galore, but he missed them all. Girlfriend went into seclusion, turning down appearances and shoots by the dozens, leaving Agent in a quandary losing her two biggest cash cows. Girlfriend was in a deep depression. Losing that Netflix role really shut her down.

Stuart was frustrated with the lack of progress, and Det. Gerarra, who was the lead on the murder case, kept the line open with Stuart, believing firmly that there was some connection. Stuart provided him with Bill's toothbrush and comb, for DNA testing. Confirming with Taj Mahal Garden, the Indian restaurant down the street, Bill had indeed ordered the Curry Chicken they found in Lallie's apartment after her brutal murder. The killer was remarkably efficient with his or her clean-up, but never noticed the paper plate of Curry Chicken that Sheldon knocked to the kitchen floor. Or maybe it was insignificant to them. In either case, Bill was a prime suspect *and* a potential victim. This was a tough case.

What they learned about Bill only added more questions than answers. Socially, he was a loner, and he spent most of his non-working time with Girlfriend. They seemed to have a strong relationship according to friends, family, colleagues and Agent, but it wasn't until a few of Bill's model clients stated he had recently sexually assaulted them did the police see cracks in his innocent-boy veneer. Agent described his mood change, and with some coaxing, Girlfriend confirmed that. Maybe he had a secret girlfriend. Maybe that secret girlfriend was Lallie. Maybe he was ill and went off to die. Maybe he just ran away from the world. You never can tell, thought Gerarra, with his 30 years of experience behind him.

Berde had told the police and Toddy that she saw Lallie and Bill leave each other's apartments some early mornings. Lallie, drunk at Berde's 86th birthday, told her that she wished Bill paid more attention to her. He'd never have dinner with her, but he'd call her in the middle of the night when Girlfriend was away, and it made Lallie feel cheap and used. She longed for a boyfriend-girlfriend dinner. Maybe she finally got that the night she was killed.

Stuart, an actor on the soap, *Nights and Days*, on cable channel 688, in which he plays Colin Jenkins, a brilliant, brash police detective, is more attractive than Bill in every conventional way. Bill was dull and forgettable. Stuart is remarkable, and even has that shining glint on his front tooth when he smiles. Girlfriend always liked being around him, and now after Bill's disappearance she's around him. They even kissed one night.

Stuart will do whatever he needs to gather intel. He doesn't trust Girlfriend. The kiss? Well, that just happened. Girlfriend has always been very attractive to him. Stuart didn't know about Professor, but he is about to find out. Girlfriend is like a steel vault; he'll never get anything from her, so he decides to date Agent and get his Det. Jenkins freak on. He is determined to find his brother.

It takes two weeks until Agent pours out her concerns about Girlfriend. She was angry, vengeful. Her meal ticket was lost, and she was genuinely concerned about Bill. Over Tom Kah Kai soup and Shrimp Pad Thai, Agent told Stuart about Professor.

"A-ha," thought, Stuart.

Back in the precinct, Gerarra pored over forensics of hair samples found in Lallie's apartment. Other than an unexplained red one, there was a hair-type fitting every one of his suspects, but the one in the plate of chicken curry found at Lallie's—that was Bill's.

TARA

Sometimes one's worst unsubstantiated fear comes true.

That's what happened with Tarly's self-fulfilling belief that her husband was dating new-widow Tara. It didn't happen right away. It took a few months, but Boss is an excellent groomer and he worked Tara from the minute he first noticed her radiant, youthful, innocent beauty at Stan's funeral.

His offer to help her was, of course, based on his own self-interest, having nothing to do with compassion or empathy. It's no wonder he and Lallie were so well-paired.

But Tara's no slouch. She knew what she was getting into. She worshipped his wealth. Coveted his wife's possessions. Loved the sky-blue and lime guest house. Adored the California King in the master bedroom in the new Greenwich house, into which Tarly had not yet moved.

As with Daveed, Boss keeps all his perceived enemies near. Free from jail, for lack of evidence, Daveed, still under suspicion, returned to his employment, saving assiduously to fund Angelica and the continued search for Josefina. It's Daveed who picks Tara up from her Bleecker Street apartment for her illicit liaisons with Boss. If it was Boss's plan to keep Daveed close to his vest, it was backfiring. The closer Daveed gets, the more information he gathers. If Boss thought Daveed knew a secret or two prior to his employment, Daveed's now a warehouse of information about Boss's misdeeds that he knows will benefit him one day. Meanwhile, Boss needs Daveed as a foil. And Daveed's more than willing, because the more Boss is present, the more suspicion with which Daveed can taint him. It's a helpful trick he learned in the Escuintla streets, along with effortless extortion and surgical beheadings.

As laser focused as she is, Tara was an initial easy mark. She loved Stan, the nerdy lug. She thought her life was over when he was murdered. She partially blamed herself for being so drunk that night and being so lost in the chaos of the evening that she forgot about Stan. Didn't realize how long he was gone. She's not good at drinking. She's had bad experiences before, walking down streets nowhere near where she intended; waking up in strange men's apartments; finding herself on a Greyhound to Sheboygan,

Wisconsin because it sounded funny at the time; calling her supervisor and telling her she loved her.

Boss had no idea what Stan might have confided in her, and whenever he had an opportunity to discuss Stan in an intimate, vulnerable moment, Tara would wisely say, "The one problem with Stan was that he was secretive about his work. He never shared anything with me." Boss was naturally relieved by her sad tale of marital concealment.

Over time, Boss, now Lallie-less, started to fall for Tara, and she was head-over-heels in love with him, he could tell. Maybe one day Kara, too, would, be a part of this relationship. He could talk anyone into anything when he put his mind to it. It's how he built his fortune, through bullshit, lies and sweet talk; interesting considering there is nothing sweet about him.

"Marry me," Tara asks on a cozy, sleep-in, rainy Sunday afternoon, in the California King in Greenwich. Tarly was in Cincinnati at her mother's funeral, a safe 688 miles away. Boss had no inclination to go. He hated the woman. He hated her ever since his mother was her mother's rival back in the butcher days. Tarly was enraged as she was chauffeured by Daveed to the airport, kids in tow. The new maid, Darlene, stayed in Sands Point to take care of Squiggles.

"Marry me," Tara says.

"She'll take me for all I have," Boss complains to his young, newly widowed mistress.

"I'm still recovering from Brenda."

It didn't matter to Tara if he married her or not. She had him where she wanted him. In bed, and Stan's very specific journal, which she has memorized, in a safe deposit box in Greenwich Village.

Oh, and that idea that Boss groomed sweet, innocent Tara from the start. Journal in hand from the day before the funeral, it was the other way around.

PART TWO

SUNLIGHT

FIRE

That was quite a year for Lallie's apartment building.

It was five years ago when her gruesome murder occurred. When Workman was paralyzed. Mr. LaRosa's heart attack. Toddy's ex falling down the stairwell. And, of course, the fatal fire in Berde's apartment that decimated Berde's, Lallie's and Bill's apartments. The rain kept the flames from collapsing the roof.

The fire started in Berde's bedroom. It's believed Admiral Jackson knocked over a space heater. How else could it have started? Berde had complained for weeks that her heat wasn't working. Harbinger never followed up, so she resorted to an old space heater. Her apartment was reduced to a charred shell, costing Harbinger more money to restore the once-cozy two-bedroom than if they had sent Super up to fix the problem. Lallie was pissed that Berde's heater was shorting her fuses.

Berde was a collector. Her apartment, filled with antiques, tchotchkes and family memorabilia was incinerated, turned to ash. Her collection of salt and pepper shakers? Powder. Her collection of ceramic elephants? Liquid. Photos of her European ancestors who survived wars, genocide, floods and famine, now all lost to time. Admiral Jackson's toys? Rubble.

One lucky happenstance, perhaps one of only two, was that Toddy filmed Berde's apartment during his interview. He had footage of all that was lost: Berde's good nature. Framed photos. The elephants. Daughter cried when Toddy sent her the interview on DVD, which was now physical documentation of Berde's rich, colorful world, filled with treasures of the past and inanimate joys of her present.

Just the day before, Berde, full of life, made plans to take a European riverboat cruise with her childhood friend, Nettie, who was turning 90 in the Fall. Berde and Nettie were quite spry and quite physically fit for nonagenarians. The two had been like sisters for eight decades. Berde's only concern was Admiral Jackson, but Big Theresa was thrilled to board him for the two weeks Berde would be sailing the Seine.

"He'd be great company for Marcellus," she said, almost begging, when Berde mentioned the trip over lunch one afternoon.

"That would be such a blessing," Berde said, relieved, brushing her hand through her kumquat-colored curls.

Big Theresa wasn't a world traveler. She'd often be entertained, however, by Nettie's wild tales about her annual trips to Italy, where Big Theresa was born 82 years ago. Theresa is imposing, weighing in at about 230 pounds, at 5'10, and while Berde liked to think her seniority in the building made her the doyenne, Big Theresa really ruled the roost. The two together, though, were a force to be reckoned with. After the fire, Big Theresa missed Berde terribly.

Every time she passed the three scarred apartments, Big Theresa would shake her head, tears streaming, blotching her heavy face powder. She'd cross herself and thank God that Doctor and Tig were vacationing in South America and Bill was MIA. She was watching Weasley and Arya. She'd touch the caution tape in front of Berde's door and whisper "God bless."

Big Theresa told Toddy, "When a death occurs in a small building like ours, there's a sickness everyone shares. It follows everyone, no matter how close they were to the victim."

Yes, Big Theresa missed Berde terribly during Berde's hospital stay which was less for her minor burns than it was for the grief she was suffering at the loss of her beloved dog.

RIP, Admiral Jackson.

When released, Berde bought her roundtrip ticket to Paris for $688 on Kayak, and flew out that evening, eager to begin her journey with Nettie. The cruise was beautiful, but no comfort, even with the companionship of her lighthearted, funny friend. She missed the Admiral.

It wasn't until now, five years later, that Berde was emotionally strong enough to get a new dog. A liver-and-white girl she named Princess Meghan. Everything was new. Dog. Refurbished apartment. This was around the time the Sessameanys moved into Lallie's.

On this bright sunny day five years later, it seems a lifetime since the fire changed

Berde's whole world, and Ghost's, who seemed to disappear forever in a puff of smoke.

SEASONS

Five years after his brother Bill's disappearance, Stuart still visits the building on Lallie's birthday, with Brother, who brings his sister's cat Sheldon, to pay their respects.

There's so much Stuart would like to share with Bill. Just like his renowned photographer brother, he, too, has become an unlikely success. Big brother Bill always thought Stuart should forgo his acting dream. Iowa wasn't the place to think of such a career. The only drama Stuart encountered there was when Bill and his unstable famous Girlfriend would visit.

Bright sunshine warms them as they place bouquets of flowers in front of Lallie and Bill's building, stems and petals soon to be peed on by Marcellus in his own ritual with their annual offerings. They hug, Stuart pets Sheldon, and he and Brother part ways until next year.

Stuart answers his cell. ""Hey, Hon. I'm on my way."

"Stuart? Oh, my god, it's Stuart," screech two teens, pulling at each other's school uniforms as Stuart walks past them.

"Hi, Girls," he says, flashing that twinkling smile.

"Oh, my God. Oh, My God, can I have your autograph?"

"Sure." He signs their notebooks.

"Can we get a selfie?"

"Sure," he says, again. He happily poses with the wildly excited twosome. And then it becomes a threesome, and four, and five. Before he knows it, there's a crowd gathered, all asking for autographs and photos.

He's used to it. It's a long way since his obscure, barely watched stint on *Nights and Days*. The tide turned when he became the newest Marvel hero. His Instagram page just hit 12 million, which makes him laugh, considering he had 26 Facebook friends when he first came to Manhattan, and four of them were his grandparents. And one was Bill. And only three were from his high school class of 688 Iowans.

On the way to Agent's office, he decides to get another bouquet.

"Hi Stu," Agent says, rushing from her desk to the photo studio down the hall, grabbing his hand and flowers, dragging him with her. "Sorry. We're in the middle of a crisis. Come with."

He's happy to tag along. He loves watching her work. All eyes in the office are on him.

The girls and the boys. And not just because he's famous.

"Sigh," Receptionist says to the visitor at her desk.

After the initial slump brought on by losing Girlfriend and Bill, her two main sources of income, Agent built her company right back up. She took Stuart on as a client and created a management division that now rivals CAA. She had little trouble getting Stuart work, and she began placing him in premium indie films. Before long, A-list directors came calling, and then there was *Seasons,* the dark-horse thriller for which he garnered Golden Globe and Oscar nominations for Best Supporting Actor. And now he's part of the Marvel universe.

What started off as a covert spy mission with Agent quickly blossomed into a full-blown love affair. A year after they met, they were engaged, and the year after that, married.

In the photo studio, Toddy's shooting a last-minute voiceover for the trailer for his new film, *The Regular Baby,* a comedy he's directing for Sony Pictures about a Satanic mix-up, starring Billy Eichner as the aforementioned mixer-upper. While Agent helped produce *688,* it was after *The Regular Baby* got picked up at Cannes and Sundance last year that she took Toddy on as a client. Now, five years after he started the documentary, it's finally about to get its Festival showing next month.

"Cut!" Toddy shouts, as he jumps up from the editing board to kiss Stuart hello.

"Hey, Toddy, it's lookin' good."

"Thanks, love, "Toddy says. "In town for a while?"

"Nope, I start a new hush-hush project in London next week," Stuart explains, as Agent is in a corner office dealing with some superstar's tantrum over her costumes.

"New James Bond, huh?"

Stuart laughs, "Could be."

"I'm definitely coming back for your premiere, though, Toddy. So exciting. You'll be showing off your Oscar nomination soon."

"Oh, Stuie, from your mouth to God's ears," exclaims Toddy.

Receptionist: "Britt, Jonathan's on line 2."

"Hi, Jonathan, we missed you at the ops conference call this morning." …

"Jonathan, see a doctor. Take as much time as you need." …

"Good. Good. Hold on a sec, Jonathan." Receptionist hands Britt a note, mouthing "important."

"I'm back. Are you feeling up to giving me a brief roundup of your properties?"…

"Good. Good"…

"Oh, no. When did he die? Oh, poor Mrs. Tiedrich. They've been tenants for 30 years. Send her a fruit basket and tell her not to worry about next month's rent. Tell her 'Britt sends her love' and I'll give her a call."…

"OK, that's great about Seattle, Jonathan. What do you think they're doing that Portland isn't?"…

"Well, let's hire that publicist for Portland as well, Jon."…

"Yes, that's even a better idea. And San Francisco, Jon, I see they're always at full occupancy. Let's not forget to get that bonus to the manager."…

"Jon, aren't the hotel kitchen staff and maid contracts up at the end of the month? The usual. Fifteen percent over cost of living."…

"Haha. Yep. That's why we have the happiest staff in the country. Nothing wrong with benevolence," Britt says with pride.

"Jon, we're scheduled to break ground in Santa Monica next month. I'll send the latest specs…."

"Take care, Jonathan, and let me know what the doctor says. Be well. Bye."

Britt buzzes Receptionist. "Please track down Daveed and ask him to come to my office.

Thanks. Oh, and your outfit today, it's killer."

The office is bustling. Business is booming. Harbinger Finance, Realty & Hotels is enjoying a financial boom ever since Britt took over the company. At 22, she's now one of the nation's most successful CEOs. When Boss was imprisoned, she took charge along with her twin brother, Chase, who's now CFO, and they operate the company with an entrepreneurial eye, but more importantly, with what Britt calls Compassionate Corporatism. She's the complete opposite of her crooked, mean-spirited father. And it's paid off in employee, client, vendor and tenant satisfaction.

Britt logs on to her email and sends out a notice to her staff: "Hey guys. It's gorgeous outdoors. Take the rest of the day off. Get some sunscreen and have a great day."

As the staff starts piling out, each one stops by her office to give a thumbs-up or just to say, "Thanks." As the office empties out, Daveed enters Britt's office. They hug.

"How's your day so far?" she asks Harbinger's apartment manager.

"Great, Britt. How's yours?"

"Busy. Wanted to let you know that Herbert Tiedrich passed away."

"Oh, no. That's sudden."

"Yes. Could you stop by and pay respects for us, this afternoon? Jonathan's taking care of everything else."

"No, problem."

"When do you think the Charleston 18th Street apartments will be ready to show?"

"We just need one more permit and we're ready to go. We're planning on showing next Thursday." Daveed always gets straight to the point.

"Awesome," Britt says, happy.

Yolande, who is Harbinger's office manager, enters Britt's office.

"I want to remind you Tomas has his school play today."

"Sure, Yolande, make sure you video it for me."

"The invoices you asked for are on my desk," Yolande reports. "ToniAnne is going to pick them up for Chase. Someone from *Forbes* called. He's working a cover feature on you, so I asked him to submit his request in writing, which he said he'd get to us tomorrow. They want to interview you next week.

"OK"

"...and Stella McCartney called about dressing you for the Met Gala. I told them that you were wearing Christian Siriani, but you'd be very interested in Stella to dress you for the banquet in your honor the following week."

"Thanks, Yolande."

"Oh, and Stefano says that Madison is acing her internship. She really likes working the hotel/hospitality end."

Britt is thrilled. Ever since their parents were incarcerated, Madison's been in her care, and the now-17-year-old being a part of the family business is quite fulfilling. It doesn't hurt that her childhood friend Maddison is working alongside her.

Harbinger: One Big Happy Family.

SHRINK

It's five years now, and Matty Lynn is preparing herself for her Big Appointment.

She'll learn if she's "cured." Cancer's never really cured she's been told, but after five years of being cancer-free, there's a good chance it won't return. Her diabetes 2 has reversed, and she's hoping for the same with her cancer.

All omens point to the positive. The sun is bright, the air crisp. People seem happy on the street. And, most importantly, Mattie feels OK. Not good, but OK. She hasn't felt "good" since first stricken with the two diseases five years ago—it was a tough year. Sometimes she wonders if her friendship with Ghost was all in her ill head.

The chemo she was on when first diagnosed had taken its toll, and she couldn't get her energy level up enough to return to Harbinger. She did some freelance writing, but the brain fog that came along with the illness and treatment began to affect that line of employment as well. Toddy hired her as a script reader and assistant, and that's how she was able to stay occupied, and not get lost in her thoughts. She didn't need to make ends meet. Her rent-controlled apartment's only $688 a month, and there's that $2.4 million she has, with no one to split it with, now that she's been ghosted by Lallie. In retrospect those were dark, intense days for her, *but today will be the beginning of a new life,* she thinks to herself as she waits for her Uber to Sloan-Kettering.

The sun feels good on her body. There have been many days when she'd lie in bed, wracked with chills. She lost a lot of weight, and her body couldn't keep up with heating her properly. Except when she would get fevers. Then she would warm up.

Waiting outside her apartment, she ties her hair in a bun, so the sun's rays can massage her neck. The warmth is invigorating. She thinks back to those cold, rainswept nights, newly diagnosed, wondering if she'd have a future that would be less bleak. A future like today.

The Uber drives her to the hospital and she waits about an hour and a half before they draw blood. Nurse, whose been through much of the journey with Matty Lynn over the past five years, pats her reassuringly on the shoulder and says, "Looks like you got a little color today."

"Yep. Sure feels good."

"You're looking good, Matty," Nurse informs her. "Let's get this blood to the lab and fingers crossed you'll get great news next week."

Matty Lynn leaves the hospital, deciding to go straight to her weekly Shrink appointment, even though it's an hour early. As she waits in Shrink's waiting room, she reads the copy of *People* that had been left on her chair. She chuckles at Toddy's photo at the opening of some *Iron-* or *Spider-* or *Ant-*man movie. She can't keep track; he's been so busy. She's been helping him coordinate next month's wide-release debut of his documentary about Lallie's murder.

She's confident that it will snag him an Oscar nomination.

She drifts, wondering what's going on in the lives of Berde, Bill, the Theresas, Mrs. LaRosa (she had heard about Mr. LaRosa's death…and she had her suspicions about how that occurred). She wondered about Boss and Harbinger. She heard the company was prospering under the supervision of Britt. She wondered about that apartment building.

"How are you today, Matty?" Shrink asks.

"I'm feeling OK. The sun's out. I'm busy with Toddy. Good week."

"So last week we discussed your friend the Doctor."

"Yeah, we kind of lost touch."

"Why?" Shrink asks.

Matty Lynn knew why. She knew that Ghost turned Doctor against her. But Shrink doesn't know about Ghost.

"I was so caught up in my illness, and she did as much as she could as my physician. I think she was so busy with her new boyfriend, Tig, and I was now under Sloan-Kettering's care, we just kind of drifted."

I wonder if they're still friends, Matty Lynn thinks, unaware that Ghost disappeared in the fire.

Even prison can feel like home when you're there long enough.

Also, after long-enough, untruths seem like truths. That's been life for Marcus over the past fifteen years at the Hope County Correctional Center in Kansas, or Nebraska…did it matter? What a lie. There's no hope here. This is a dead end.

And so it seemed to Marcus, until he heard from a random documentarian five years ago, when Lallie died, to ask him to participate in a documentary about her murder. After ten years of incarceration, it wouldn't be a lie to say Marcus was thrilled by the news of Lallie's grotesque death. After all, she was responsible for his grotesque life.

Surprisingly, Marcus didn't think about Lallie in these fifteen years in prison, even though she was the cause. There were dark nights when reality was blurred and he, too, wasn't sure any more about what happened that day Lallie was beaten.

Marcus liked getting visitors. Unlike the rest of the prison, the visitors area had window bars, through which the otherwise unattainable sunlight snuck its snakelike rays into the cavernous meeting room. It's even more gratifying than his hour in the yard, because there are civilians surrounding him here. And he's still holding tightly to that human part of himself.

Today's visitor sits across from him, a 5'10" ball of energy, splash of dyed-blonde pompadour resting on a bush of brown meticulously groomed hair. He looked like a NYC filmmaker, Marcus thought.

Toddy holds out his hand, "Nice to meet you."

"Nice to meet you, too, Sir" Marcus responds respectfully.

Toddy's nervous; Marcus is a big "get." He hasn't spoken to anyone about Lallie since he became Inmate #7954908, C Building, Cell #688. He hasn't given one interview, nor has he discussed the case with family or friends. He's lucky in one respect, his family and friends' support for him has remained indefatigable and resolute. Fifteen years in now, their support's unwavering.

"I'm curious," Toddy asks, "why speak with me?"

Marcus doesn't really know.

"Something about your letter," he answers.

Toddy drives straight to the point. Get the most uncomfortable questions out there first. He doesn't want to build up to them because he has no idea if Marcus will freeze or bolt from his queries.

"Marcus, tell me? Did you beat Lallie?"

Taken aback, Marcus doesn't know how to answer.

"Well, I'm in prison for it, aren't I?"

"That doesn't mean much to me," Toddy says. "There's lots of innocent people in prison."

Marcus has been studying law. After getting his GED in prison (he was one month from graduating high school with honors when he was convicted) he received his online BA from the University of Kansas, in communications. With nothing else to do but read, he taught himself everything he could about the law. If he were a free man, without a felony record, he'd take— and pass—the bar. As determined as he is to better himself in prison, he's equally determined not to give himself false hope, so every time the thought of an appeal or working with some Innocence Project flits through his over-active mind, he brushes it aside. By now he would have graduated Yale, had several years building his career, nurturing a family, and being in love, and loved. But instead, he's here savoring these stolen minutes, captive, behind concrete and bars, with this strange gay kid from New York City who makes movies.

"Marcus. I've been conducting a lot of research and interviewing a lot of people, and I think that Lallie might have beaten herself up that day. Is that what happened?"

The hoops Toddy had to jump through to attain this interview were many. Lallie's been dead for five years, and it's taken all this time to be granted this interview. He's determined to get to the bottom of this.

An errant sun ray, muted slightly by the palpable din of the visitors center struck Marcus' cheek, illuminating it in almost biblical sheen. It's warmth, or even perhaps its celestial deep meaning, jolted Marcus, because after 15 years, he was suddenly ready to talk.

DREAMLAND

After the fire, Doctor decided it was time to move. Lallie was no longer there, and it was just too small for her and Tig, newly minted as a committed couple during their Bahamas trip.

"Marry me," she asked him impulsively while sunbathing in front of the horizon line where the ocean's aquamarine met the azure blue of the sky, as the fiery, blood-orange sun set in the distance.

"Yeah, OK," he laughed, and it was set. They'd be a couple. A month after they returned from the Bahamas, they moved to a small town in Westchester, Sleepy Hillside or Merrytown, something whimsically pastoral and fairytale-like, and that's how the last five years have played out for them since they met. A lot can happen in five years, and both grew tired of their respective jobs, and quit. They opened up a jazz club in Merry Hillside or Sleepytown.

Dreamland.

Five years ago, after months of Lallie bad-mouthing Matty Lynn, Doctor decided to confront Matty Lynn about the awful charges made against her. It was five years after the fire, before Doctor believed Lallie might be gone for good, and a week after Matty Lynn's Shrink appointment, when they ran into each other at the hospital. After initial awkward pleasantries, Matty Lynn, who looked skeletal and weak, asked Doctor, "What happened? Why did you pull away from me?"

Doctor told her all. Matty Lynn was aghast. She had heard Lallie tell similar stories about
Tig, Marcus and others who were "abusive" to her, and now *she* was the subject of those stories.

She invited Doctor to the hospital cafeteria where they could talk, and Doctor obliged.

"I'm shocked by what you're telling me," Doctor says, "and I believe everything you're saying. It all makes sense now. Especially hearing about the stories Lallie told you about Tig."

Doctor had never seen that violent side of him, and that file of charges that Hammerstein threw at him five years ago while he was being interrogated. Doctor believes Tig's explanation. The sinister side of Lallie came through loud and clear during their chat, which evolved into weekly lunches, and eventually weekend visits to Merry Sleepy as Matty Lynn's health began to slowly improve.

Matty Lynn lives a simple life. She wonders, *So, what to do with this $2.4 million sitting in a 5th Avenue safe deposit box?* Well, invest part in Dreamland.

The partnership between the three has been so successful and amicable, they've been talking about setting up other Dreamlands— one in Atlanta, the other in Philly. Tig, who was more than happy to put his psychiatric practice to rest, is in charge of the expansion. Doctor, who everyone now lovingly calls, "Doc," runs the day-to-day (really, night-to-night) at the club. She loves nothing more than lounging in a chair in the dim light and listening to some sultry chanteuse scat her little heart out, or some local music teacher wail away on the sax, or enjoy the weekend headliners, whose albums her father used to play religiously, while she voraciously devoured the latest pop songs.

This was the life. During the day, she and Tig would sit in their luxe backyard engrossed in accounting and paperwork, birds twittering all around them, the brush of the leaves as they sway in the early summer wind, the syncopation of the small beasties scampering through the woods, the pop and ripple of fish in the pond that separates their property from their neighbor. They are living the jazz they sell at night in the natural way, during the day.

Dreamland is no slouch of a club, with a capacity of 688 (570 seated; 118, standing at the bar), this renovated barn has become the "It" venue, and the bill of fare has expanded. An acclaimed regional theater, the last two "Best Musical" Tony winners incubated here. Lincoln Center runs a "Dreamland" series here. Toddy films a weekly PBS program, *Live from Dreamland* that airs on PBS here. Tig and Doc married here. Matty Lynn recoups here. For this group of friends, since the murder, the last five years has seemed like dreamland.

The Regal Theater is filled, 688 audience members: principals in the case, film buffs, distributors, groupies, true-crime buffs, and a judging panel who have seen all the entries and will determine the event's "Best of Festival" award. They're all anxiously anticipating the long-awaited debut of Toddy's documentary about Lallie's murder. The film project has had many starts and stops, like the case it documents, and thanks to those challenges and delays, a killer was revealed, and a mystery solved.

Red carpet. Check. Wave to the crowd. Check. Smile for the paparazzi. Check.

Butterflies in the stomach. Check. Handsome on his arm. Check.

As the end credits roll, and the cheering continues, Toddy stands and acknowledges the

praise.

"Bravo!"

"Bravo!"

This was a bittersweet and hard-fought triumph. He would talk about it during the Q&A which will start in 15 minutes. Toddy bends down, kisses Handsome to his right and Matty Lynn to his left, both beaming, walks up to the stage where he's joined by Det. Gerarra, Agent, Yolande and Daveed. Each, making a great impact in the film, are greeted by cheers and whistles as they're announced. The Q's and the A's come rapidly, and with great zeal.

Q: "Toddy, it's been five years since the murder, why did it take so long for the film to come out?"

A: "Funding. I always had a little help from my friends and family, and I had a few producers along the way, but they all flaked out, stringing me along sometimes for years—and one day, out of the blue, I received a cashier's check in the mail for 200K, from an anonymous donor [Matty Lynn wiggles nervously in her seat] and that allowed me to do enough filming to snag a distributor, and the rest as they say…" The audience laughs. They are eating up every Q and every A.

Q: "Det. Gerarra, you say in the film that you are proud of Toddy for helping to solve this murder. Do you think that's the job of a documentarian or the police?" The audience oohs and ahhs.

A: "Listen," the no-nonsense cop responds, "do I wish our guys solved this? Sure. We were close. But Toddy did his homework, and he deserves all the credit for this." The audience cheers. "It's not about credit. It's about solving the case." Applause.

Q: "Daveed (the audience stands, shouting approval, fist pumping). Daveed, your story's like a whole other movie in this documentary. Your search for your daughter is heartbreaking. All along you're a prime suspect in a murder case. Do you resent the cops?"

A: "No, man. Not at all. Look at me, man. I even think I look like the first person you should suspect." The audience laughs. "Seriously, though, when people see me, they see a tattooed gangbanger immigrant who's up to no good. And it's not just me. Look at who the original suspects were. Me, Tig, you notice something about us? We're outcasts. We don't look like Boss or luxe Tarly. This film shows, in twisting *esplendor*, how society infects the outsider. Nah, I don't resent it. I expect it." Cheers and hoots.

A: "I need to say something here," Gerarra interjects, "and I think it was made clear in the film, you were a suspect, Daveed, because you disappeared. If you had been around, it would have been a different story." The audience adds some friendly booing, and hand-waving shooing his answer from the universe.

A: "There's even more to it, Detective," Toddy interrupts. "It's because of his reserve and his disinterest in interacting with a class of people he had no interest in. Same with Tig. He wanted nothing to do with polite society, so he's a target. Because they appeared like outsiders they attracted suspicion, while the likes of Boss, in his suit and tie, went about without notice that night." Cheers. Tig stands up and comically bows to high-fives from those around him.

Agent: "On that note, let's take a 15-minute break. But before we do, we have a little surprise for Toddy."

Handsome walks on stage, gets on one knee….

After the intermission, and Toddy's gushing marriage acceptance, the judges announce the Festival Awards: The Best of Festival Award goes to *688*, and its director, Toddy.

The Q&A reconvenes.

There's only a half-hour left, and a hundred more questions.

"Let's get back to Daveed's side story," emcee Agent announces. "It's kind of mind-boggling to think that because of this murder, and because he was a suspect, it all conspired in a way to enable him to retrieve his daughter, who I think is in the audience. Josefina?"

The shy 8-year-old stands and waves, with her proud mother at her side. The audience is on their feet, screaming their approval. Misty eyes, everywhere. Daveed tears up, and Gerarra hands him a handkerchief.

"If he had not been arrested, and told his story to Gerarra, everything that went into motion to help find Josefina probably would never have happened. All the human cruelty that enveloped her was soon washed away by the goodwill of the principals in tonight's film. You saw how Gerarra got law enforcement involved. How Stuart... (delighted screeches erupt from the audience) and I mobilized the entertainment community who helped promote her plight on social media. Britt and Harbinger Finance, Realty & Hotels helped fund the legal fight to return her to her parents. And Toddy's videos helped her story go viral. There's goodness in this world fighting the unspeakable evil we are encountering." Applause.

Q: "How's Berde doing?" Audience starts chanting, "Berde!" "Berde!" "Berde!"

A: "She's here," Toddy announces. "Berde, say 'Hi'?" Berde stands. Triumphantly, eating up the attention, waving like royalty.

Q: "Yolande... (Cheers, again, break out. After all, she helped solve the case.) Yolande, do you feel like the hero in all of this?"

A: Yolande laughs, then a long, intentional, overly dramatic "Uhmmm...yes!" The energized audience agrees. "I was just doing what's right."

Q: "Yolande, did you ever think Boss was the murderer?

A: "To be honest. Yes. But everything changed the night I helped Miss Tarly remove that wig."

Q: "Are you glad Boss is in prison?"

A: "Yes, he cheated a lot of people. He thought just because I was the maid, or Latina, or a woman, that I was invisible. He would wheel and deal right in front of me. I was one of those invisibles that Daveed was talking about, and sometimes when you make someone invisible, they become dangerous." The audience gives her a standing O.

A: Gerarra: "Yolande, in the film, when Tara produces Stan's journal with all Boss's crooked financials to Toddy, and you were then able to confirm each point, that was another turning point in the case. Money laundering, bank fraud, RICO, you name it, we had Boss dead-to-rights. I think we also owe a debt of gratitude to Tara. Tara, you here?" Tara stands, absorbing the adulation of the cheering crowd. Her and Boss's 5-year-old, Jenny, is home, asleep.

Q: "Yolande, you made it clear that you didn't like Tarly? If you liked her would you have still put two and two together?"

A: "That's a great question. I don't know the answer because I can't imagine any situation where I'd like her. But the fact is, I didn't like either of them and I was suspicious of both from Day-One. The wig was the final straw. I had to tell someone. I knew she was at Lallie's apartment that night, and I knew she was capable of outrageous jealousy. So, I was lucky to have Toddy visit when he did."

Q: "Toddy, what did it feel like when you realized who the real killer was? It was chilling in the film when you discussed it, but can you tell us what was going through your mind?"

A: "I had done so many interviews. I would sit every night with Matty Lynn and go over every new puzzle piece. Things started adding up. Tig's story. And then Marcus' remarkable interview. It was after I spoke with Marcus, and I came home and just vomited out his details to Matty Lynn, when we both looked at each other and said, 'Shit, Lallie killed herself.'"

IGNITE

Spark. Spark. Sizzle, spark.
Flicker.
Ignite.
Blazing.
Dreamland is consumed by flames. Raging.

Fortunately, the venue is closed because Doc, Tig, Matty Lynn and Toddy are all at the premiere of *688* and, probably now, the after-party at TokyoBar.

It is three alarms, fire trucks coming from Pleasant Hollow, Merry Village, Sleepy Hillside, whatever. The suburban silence rattled by screeching sirens and flashing lights leading a futile trail to Dreamland.

Partygoers looking north toward the Hudson from TokyoBar see gray billows playing hide and seek with twinkling stars that had been so proudly bursting through the deep purple sky only minutes prior.

At Dreamland, the air's thick with embers and crackle, splintering through the night's serenity. Firemen, choking, resort to oxygen breaks, reviving their lungs enough to get them through the veil of heat and cinders. This repository of beauty is now a combustible time bomb. The roof caves. Hennessy bottles crack. Dewar's, Remy, Beefeater, Bacardi, Cîroc Ten. Then the bottled beers explode, glasses and mugs all melting away. The Steinway, charred, and glowing. The ivories blacken and crackle, cremated. Spotlights splinter shards across the night sky in the roofless skeleton. All senses assaulted, as every object emits its own particular burning smell.

The box office, rubble. The cash registers, deformed, indistinguishable from the corrupted surfaces upon which they rested.

At TokyoBar, all is celebratory. Toddy's enjoying his engagement and long-in-the-making success. Britt, Chase and Madison, successfully separating themselves from their parents' offenses, have taken the past five years' revelations, particularly the disclosures of *688,* in stride. Just that afternoon, Britt was selected CEO of the Year by *Fortune* magazine, so she and her siblings and friends have an additional reason to celebrate. Britt might be the face of Harbinger Finance, Realty & Hotels, but Chase and Madison are enjoying basking in their sister's and company's successes, and the good will of their stockholders and staff. Maddison, who's been dating Madison for three years now, falls naturally into the family's united front. Daveed and Monica, are dancing with Josefina. It's rare to see Daveed so outgoing, and fun-filled. It is a relief being fully exonerated. The cloud that followed him was a burden.

The focus on the dancefloor, of course, is little Josefina, looking beautiful in her rose-colored party dress, with matching bow in her long black hair. Five years ago, in a detention camp, ripped from her parents, she could never have imagined this night. And how exciting was it when her daddy was introduced to the audience at the movie premiere and everyone clapped for him and cheered when he brought her on stage with him. Josefina, through this film, has become a symbol of all that's good and bad with the world, and any 8-year-old would be reveling in this joyous night along with a bunch of equally happy grownups.

Berde, Nettie and Big Theresa, picked up by stretch limo, are belles of the ball. Dancing with all the handsome young men and trying food they never ate before—blackened alligator egg rolls! Stuart and Agent are always the center of attention; he for his fame and she for being the provider of fame. They're overjoyed to have Bill by their side. And alive. He's enjoying a busman's holiday as the after-party's exclusive photographer. Brother is there with Sister-in-Law, after braving through what must have been a painful two hours of film. Yolande and Tara receive standing ovations when they arrive: the heroines of *688*. Gerarra, who's made his amends with Tig and Daveed, is letting loose as best he can, hobnobbing awkwardly. Tig and Doc, who produced this event are busy being not busy. It's a nice change from the demands of Dreamland.

And Matty Lynn is celebrating the good news. She is, indeed, and without question, cancer-free.

All this as Dreamland burns.

Spark. Spark. Sizzle, spark.

Flicker.

Ignite.

Blazing.

Dreamland is consumed by flame, cinders and ash.

There was no accelerant. Except for maybe the premiere of *688*, and the revelations that were revealed after all these years. Fire, raging.

Lallie is erupting as she tends to the blaze she started at Dreamland.

JOSEFINA

It's been five years and two months since Daveed was brought in for questioning, a prime suspect, and at that time the only suspect, in Lallie's murder.

Today, he leans back in his leather chair, in his corner office at Harbinger Finance, Realty & Hotels, where he's the manager of its apartment buildings, with a staff of 123 working underneath him, making more money in a month than he'd earn in a lifetime hustling in restaurants, bars, opening doors and driving limos. But it's the respect he's earned that makes him so pleased. There have been adjustments, for sure; being amiable is the one he's worked on the hardest. In the five-plus years, employed in a positive environment like Britt's Harbinger, the daunting task was easier than it seemed it would be. Naturally a nice guy, all Daveed needed to do was let his guard down a bit.

Five years ago was a traumatic turning point in his life. Seesawing between defending his freedom and concentrating on the thing most important to him, finding and reuniting with 3-year-old Josefina. Thanks to Monica's strength throughout their ordeal, Angelica's tireless advocacy and the financial help of Britt and Tara, Josefina was found and returned to them, a year later. Today they're all American citizens. It was a long mentally and physically exhausting haul, but as they wrapped their arms around their daughter all was well with the world. Monica, through choking tears, crying "*Gracias, Dios*"; " *Bendícenos a todos*" and "*Mi bebe ya regreso,*" not letting Josefina out of her tight embrace and Daveed standing awestruck by this beautiful young girl returned to him.

It wasn't until they realized that it wasn't just shyness that was preventing their once-babbling baby from expressing herself, both verbally and physically. She stood in place, accepting everyone's adoration, not uttering a word, or showing emotion. She had become mute and drained of emotion. Tara immediately set up an appointment with the best team of doctors specializing in trauma, and within a year of her return, she began exhibiting more normal behavior. She has barely spoken since, however. Now, at 8 years old, she makes her needs and concerns plainly known, but not through speech. She's been muted.

Daveed finishes off his office work, drops by Britt's office to say goodbye, and is driven to his spacious home in Queens in the company car, by his chauffeur Leonid. He invites Leonid for dinner, but Leonid has family obligations in Brooklyn, and politely declines. Josefina sees the car arriving and runs across their well-manicured, beautifully landscaped acre-long front yard to greet him. Her rescue mutt, Bingo, is at her heels. She jumps in Daddy's arms and he swings her around. She laughs uncontrollably. She has learned to laugh.

"*Ven, mi princesa*, we have soccer practice." Daveed has been coaching Josefina's soccer team, for two years now. Soccer saved him back home in Guatemala. It taught him camaraderie, teamwork and determination. He loved the sport, regretting growing up too fast in Escuintla, graduating quickly from soccer fields to gang turf. He named Josefina's team, The 688s, after the Seiscientos Ochenta y Ocho, the 688 people from his town who died in the violence that sprouted around him like weeds. He told Josefina and her teammates that they're named for heroes from his hometown. So distant from knowing about the real world, here in Queens, without understanding the depth of the moniker, they're proud to carry the name.

Josefina has become a poster child for the immigrant cause. Her return, celebrated around the world, and her journey with mutism is followed by millions, ranging from Central American peasants to European royalty. Rock stars, supermodels, athletes, have all taken up the cause, and follow Josefina's story, which Monica shares daily on Instagram.

Daveed and Josefina are joined by Monica, who's rarely ever out of physical reach of Josefina since her return five years ago. Bingo goes back indoors, and they're off to the game against The Lion Kings.

On the ride over, Monica, is bursting, not knowing when's the best time to break the exciting news that she's pregnant.

JENNY

   With Stan's journal in hand, Tara got Boss to marry her.

   What did he have to lose? He was in a no-win situation. Rock.
Hard place. Accepting her deal, he'd be free from her implied
blackmail and once married, Tara couldn't testify against him. He'd
also be rid of his other baggage, Tarly. Hmm, maybe it's win-win
after all.

   Jenny coming along secured the new arrangement. Pregnant,
Tara insisted that she and Boss marry before their daughter's birth.
Boss knew the cops suspected him in Lallie's death, and the Feds
were following his finances. Putting his money in Jenny's name
seemed like a good idea. To both him and Tara.

   Things didn't work out quite the way Boss had hoped. Tara
managed to manipulate many of his assets into her own. Tarly
couldn't fight her, because much of the financial fraud for which
they were being investigated was done in marital union, under both
their names, plus prosecutorial eyes were on her as well for a wide
spectrum of crimes.

   When Boss was indicted, and pilloried in the press, Tara realized
it would be an advantageous time for her to gain public sympathy
and to cash in. So, she divorced him. Facing more charges than
Bernie Madoff and Paul Manafort combined, Boss had to acquiesce
to Tara's demands. Basically, all his fortune that wasn't due his kids,
and full custody of Jenny, who was now financially secure for
life…and beyond, went to Tara. Thanks for the sperm, Boss.

   Tara worked closely with both Det. Gerarra and Toddy, freely
sharing the damning contents of Stan's meticulous secret journal.
Case over, Tara turned her attention to charity. She started a 501c3
non-profit, Families United, to help reunite immigrants with their
children who had been severed from them at the southern U.S.
border and to also aid those from "shithole countries" to reunite with
their families. Jenny's birth gave her new purpose. She couldn't
imagine being separated from her, and it inspired her to use her
newfound wealth for good. Still close friends with Matty Lynn, she
continued offering to pay for medical expenses and anything else to
help ease her financial situation since her illness was preventing her
from working fulltime, but Matty Lynn always rejected her kind

offers. As close as she was to Matty Lynn, Tara didn't know about the $2.4 million. Nobody did. Not even Matty Lynn's best friend Toddy.

In the five years since Tara met Boss, she and her stepdaughter Britt had become close friends and business associates, often pooling their resources to help bring immigrant families together. Partnered, Families United and Harbinger helped Daveed find Josefina. They enabled a young Yemeni man to remain in the U.S. long enough to donate a kidney to his ailing grandfather, who was a citizen. They paid for all hospital expenses as well. They helped a young girl remain in Tennessee with her aunt and uncle after it was discovered that her Somali parents, now both dead of AIDS, were undocumented. ICE attempted to remove her from the only home and family she's known and return to her to Somalia, even though she no longer had relatives there and even though she was born in the U.S. Now Tara and Britt are devoting their time to help all of the Lost Children reunite with their parents, whose information has been suspiciously "mislaid" by the government.

This is Tara's cause. Outraged that scores of pregnant Russian women, who were staying at Trump properties in the U.S., would give birth here so their children would be Americans, the hypocrisy was obvious. Russians are white. This became Tara's driving mission, and luckily, she had the money to support it.

Jenny, now 5, is about to start pre-kindergarten. She's a precocious little thing, a prodigy on piano. Where the talent comes from is anyone's guess, but the girl's destined for great success if music's the course she eventually takes.

Meanwhile, Tarly seethes in prison, locked within concrete and iron bars, with nothing to ruminate over other than Lallie, that scheming widow Tara, and that little punk 5-year-old who has all her money.

After the fire, Doctor moved out of her apartment, and the Sessameanys moved in.

They've lived there now for five years. John, a professional mixed martial-arts fighter, his wife Sally, a cashier at Whole Foods, and their 7-year-old son, Garrett. Money is tight for them, but they manage. Life is sweet, except for Sally's Ex, who refuses to move on, calling her, harassing her, every couple of days. Ex doesn't seem to know the meaning of "no."

The Sessameanys love the freedom of this apartment. They had been living in Sally's parents mansion in Chevy Chase, Maryland, and those years weren't easy.

Father and Mother were always supportive, but even as a child, Sally could not abide by their politics. Father was the head of Maryland's Conservative party, and Mother, a successful lawyer, was one of the lead counsels for Monsanto, of toxic Roundup notoriety, now part of Bayer. When people sued because their loved ones got lymphoma from Roundup exposure from spraying their gardens or eating Cheerios, it was Mother who fought the 688 victims in court. Not to mention the millions of people with irritable bowels brought on by Monsanto's genetically modified food. Sally, a strict vegan, appreciates her parents' generosity to her, their only child, but she can no longer tolerate living in their orbit. Fortunately, her friend Little Theresa, mentioned a fairly inexpensive two-bedroom apartment opening in her building, down the hall from her.

Little Theresa and Sally were best friends throughout their lives, despite distance separating them at times, and Sally was thrilled to move close to her lifelong confidante. It was Sally who gave King Kong to Little Theresa, when her own cat, Godzilla, gave birth to a litter of three: Mothra, Rodan and King Kong. When King Kong went missing (bad, bad Lallie), Sally brought Mothra to replace her. Godzilla and Rodan reside with Mother and Father, monsters of a different type.

Little Theresa is Garrett's godmother and she babysits for him when John is training and Sally's at work. Garrett enjoys Little Theresa's company immensely. While he's in school, she attends to her freelance writing and social media influencing, for which she gets paid a tidy sum. Always dressed in black, with severe bangs and a sharp-cut hairdo, her ebony hair almost shining blue, Garrett teases her, calling her Wednesday, after both of their favorite Addams Family character.

"What a beautiful day for the park," Little Theresa suggests, and Garrett, fresh from school, agrees. Once there, Garrett's handed sunscreen, the sun is shining bright, and he's soon off to play with his many friends who populate the park after school. Little Theresa takes out her iPad and completes a story she is writing for Vulture on the #MeToo movement in the healthcare sector. Feeling someone's watching her, she repeatedly looks over her shoulder. But there's no one. That she sees.

Before depositing Garrett back home, Little Theresa tends her tiny garden in the front of their building, with the 7-year-old's assistance. It hasn't rained in ages and the flowers need some extra care. They're thirsty as hell. She and Garrett go upstairs to her apartment, fill two watering cans, the black one for her, and the Batman one for him, and they return to the garden.

Before the fire, the garden would never thrive, as if some evil force was draining the life from it. But strangely, ever since the fire, the garden is flourishing. And that's good news for Garrett, the precocious junior environmentalist.

Again, Little Theresa gets that feeling of being watched, and instead of turning around, she inconspicuously picks up the trowel, spits on it, wiping the dirt away, and raises it enough to view what's behind her. The image is blurred, but there's no mistaking it. It's Ex. Little Theresa looks at her watch, pretends she's late for something, packs up her garden tools, and scuttles Garrett back into the building.

Later that night, she tells John and Sally about it out of hearing range of Garrett.

"He scares the hell out of me," Sally says tearfully.

"Me too," says John Sessameany, the tough mixed-martial-arts fighter.

CASTAWAY

    Despite a childhood filled with piano and vocal lessons, Matty Lynn, who has never written or performed a song in her life, sits down at Toddy's Yamaha and plinks out a mournful melody. Lyrics tease slowly and soon they blossom in stanzas, bridges and choruses. The theme returns in a rush, months after Matty Lynn finally shared her mutual experience with Doctor about their now almost-inconceivable mutual relationships with Ghost. Matty Lynn was finally able to put into indelible words and song what she was, for five years, unwilling to impart to her family and friends, about her lost intense friendship with Ghost.

        "Must be a safer way to end this business now
        Must be a safer to take this final bow
        I am a castaway
        Driftwood on a beach
        There must be a safer way to be cast out of reach

        "Castaway
        Passed, away from your side
        Castaway
        Just a spark of fire
        Just a castaway

        "This is a comedy
        A comedy of errors
        This is a comedy
        Like a peacock without feathers

        "I am castaway
        A play without a plot
        There must be a safer way to be cast about

        "Castaway
        Passed away from your side
        Castaway
        Just a spark of fire

Just a castaway

"I am a castaway
A play without a plot
Must be a safer way to be cast about

"Castaway
Passed, away from your side
Castaway
Just a spark of fire
Just a castaway."

"Wow, that's beautiful," Toddy exclaims from the kitchen when Matty Lynn finishes it.

"Let's make a video," he suggests.

Matty Lynn, feeling stronger by the day, thinks about it.

"Come on, Matty Lynn. You're beautiful, you have a great singing voice and this song is outrageously good. Let's make a video, and make it go viral. You'll be the next Taylor Swift." Toddy, whose whole world centered around Lallie for the past five years, has no idea this song is about her.

"Where'd that all come from?" he asks his roommate.

"Artists never reveal their secrets," she jokes.

For weeks, Toddy and Matty Lynn work on perfecting the video of "Castaway." At Agent's, they work in the studio with top session players Toddy hired. Agent goes all out with make-up and styling. Stuart's got a cameo. Everyone's thrilled Matty Lynn's seeming healthier by the day. Toddy perfects his script till the very last second.

It's a beautiful day in Central Park. The sun's shining brightly; filtered through Toddy's cameras and the sun's blonde rays, there's the illusion of gold dust flurrying around Matty Lynn at her piano. Filming goes on without a hitch, and the session players are so professional, the music is finished in one take. Now comes the editing, and Toddy is immersed in it. He's been busy in film and TV, with great success, but this is his first music video, and he's ecstatic about it. He does make a point of reminding everyone that "Although this is my first music video, it's not like I haven't been hounded to do others. Just ask Adam Lambert and Cardi B."

Agent gets to work having all her influencers simultaneously Instagramming the now completed video. "Castaway" becomes all the rage, and Matty Lynn's bluesy vocals are immediately compared to Dusty Springfield and everyone wants a piece of her—record labels, producers, concert promoters and headliners. It's the age of technology and her fame comes faster than the 688-class nuclear-powered fast attack submarine, USS Los Angeles. That fast.

"Castaway" tops every music chart, iTunes, Spotify, *Billboard*, and is omnipresent on radio. You'd spend five minutes in Panera or Starbucks and be bound to hear it. Forty-five minutes, you'd hear it twice. Put your car radio on scan, and there's a good possibility you will catch it on at least six stations. The video: almost 46 million views in its first two weeks. The video, Matty Lynn, and Toddy received a total of eight MTV Video Music Award nominations, including "Video of the Year." There's talk of a Grammy nomination as well.

All on a wistful whim to make sense of what might have been just an irresolvable fantasy.

Bill returned from the dead five years after Lallie's death. When he was confident it was safe.

At first, he thought he'd wait for Girlfriend to leave Manhattan, and he'd return, but those tranquil, meditative days in the healing New Mexico sun were a stronger siren call than tempting his fate with unstable Girlfriend.

A month after the murder, Girlfriend returned to Bill's apartment under Stuart's keen supervision. Reclaiming her possessions, a rumble was heard in a closet, the one sharing a wall with Lallie's apartment. Unfortunately, Girlfriend was in that very closet when a 75-pound barbell was somehow shaken from its resting place on the closet's top shelf, falling, crushing more than half of the 26 bones in each foot. Fracturing enough bones to take her out of commission for a long while. She was taken by ambulance to the hospital, and that was the last Girlfriend was seen by Stuart. She moved in with her cousin Bernadette in Gainesville after learning that Southern college towns were more handicapped-friendly than a bustling city. She and her wheelchair would fare better there. And the further she'd get from Det. Gerarra's peering, suspicious eyes, the better. How far her world had crumbled over the past year.

Never psychologically stable, the stress of her high-profile job grew to be more than her fragile personality could handle. She enjoyed being in the public eye, but the exigencies had become too much—always in demand, always in the spotlight. A year after Lallie's death, Girlfriend was extradited to New York for questioning after it was determined that she had indeed been in Lallie's apartment the night of the murder, despite her vigorous denials. Berde had seen her, and there was forensic hair and fingerprint evidence.

Five years ago, Bill was ready to break up with Girlfriend. Her jealousy contaminating their relationship and his work. It wasn't that he was so much in love with Lallie, he had grown used to her, but he needed a change from Girlfriend, as beautiful as she was.

The night of the murder, Bill set his curry chicken aside and answered the knock at his door.

A man he didn't know, bearded, with dark, brooding eyes, and wet, blond hair stuck onto his forehead, greeted him. It was a stormy night and he apparently had no umbrella.

"Bill?"

"Yeah?"

"You have a minute for me? I have some interesting information I'd like to share with you."

Bill, untrusting, continued to hold the door slightly ajar. "What is it? Who are you?"

"My name's Carlisle. You have a minute to hear a recording?"

Bill, intrigued. "OK, play it."

"Not in the hall," Carlisle whispered to him. "Trust me, man."

Gut instinct told Bill he could trust him. Interesting, considering Carlisle was a hitman.

Ushered into the apartment, Carlisle removes his phone from the inside jacket pocket and plays a recording. It's Girlfriend, offering him $688 to kill Bill and Lallie.

Bill knew Girlfriend was unhinged, but he never expected this.

"So, you here to kill me?" Bill asks, stunned into inaction.

"No, brother, I'm here to warn you. I turned her down, and I wouldn't be surprised if she decides to do this herself."

They talk details for a few minutes and then part ways, Carlisle back into the rain, and

Bill into an entire new mindset. He calls Lallie. He needs to warn her.

"I'm coming over. Did'ya eat yet?"

"No." She lies.

"I'll bring over some curried chicken."

"That sounds perfect," Lallie coos.

As he walks to Lallie's, he's already devised his getaway plan. There's a retreat, Tranquil Adobe, in Santa Fe, that he discovered during a recent assignment, where people go to "disappear." Its privacy policy rivals HIPPA. There's no way anyone will find him there. Short term, long term, he was prepared for either. He'd wait it out until Girlfriend would no longer be a threat. He knew how tenacious she was; once something's on her mind, there's no stopping her.

He had to disappear.

When Bill later learned about Lallie's murder, he believed with all his heart that Girlfriend killed Lallie that night.

John and Sally Sessameany turn on Netflix, a bit wary.

"You sure you wanna do this?" John asks.

"Yeah, sure, why not? The worst is we'll have nightmares and wanna move," she responds, chuckling nervously.

With Garrett at Little Theresa's, they cuddle on the couch and select *688*, Toddy's award-winning documentary about, well, their apartment. Glued to the film, they point out renovations that have been made and wonder what Lallie was like as they enter her world. Poor girl. Everyone initially described her as innocent and sweet.

The couple brace for the murder scene re-enactment. Toddy hired unknowns because he didn't want someone's acting history to color the story: "Oh, Dakota Fanning's so good as Matty Lynn." He wanted clean slates to easily morph into their real-life counterparts. That was one of the successes of the film.

Bill enters Lallie's apartment with Indian food and wine, which they share. He informs her about Girlfriend's attempt to hire a hitman. Lallie's hoping Bill stays the night, but he leaves after dinner, warning her to be careful. He says he's leaving town and suggests she do the same. When he leaves, her personality changes. It's chilling. The film's earlier interviews with Tig, Marcus (which is heartbreaking; a lost life) and others, describing Lallie's double personality and her vindictive self-hurting is unnerving. And this personality change they see when Bill leaves her apartment is darkly foreboding.

After Bill leaves, Lallie's self-harm obsession surfaces. She wants to punish him. And Girlfriend. And Boss. And Tig. And that unfriendly Doorman. And whoever else ever slighted her. It's a brutal scene, difficult even for John, who deals in blood sport, to watch. He winces as Lallie punches, beats and batters herself. At one point, she bashes her head against the bathroom wall so hard that Berde's medicine cabinet moves off-center, frightening both Berde and Admiral Jackson.

The head-bashing makes Lallie nauseous and she lies down in her tub, setting off seizures. She dies of brain trauma minutes later. Lallie is her own murderer.

It's midnight, rain is pelting Lallie's window as Boss enters the apartment, sees Lallie lifeless, and leaves as stealthily as he arrived. Fifteen minutes later, Bill returns to Lallie's apartment because he left his phone there. Maybe they'll have sex one last time, he thinks. That'll make her happy. He has her key from when he once cat sat for Sheldon.

John and Sally are yelling at the TV screen, "Don't go in! Don't go in!"

When Bill sees her dead, he's sure Girlfriend's responsible. He leaves in a rush, forgetting to lock her door, which makes it easy for Girlfriend to enter a half-hour later, after not getting a response at Bill's.

"That bastard must be with Lallie," she grumbles as she storms to Lallie's apartment with murder on her mind. But as she enters, she realizes someone's gotten there before her. Not realizing Lallie killed herself.

She takes a bottle of wine from the kitchen that she recognizes as Bill's and the wine glass without lipstick and leaves the incriminating items conspicuously keeping the apartment door ajar.

Girlfriend furtively leaves, taking the stairs after observing the elevator reaching the sixth floor. A woman in a soaking-wet, rust-red wig, looking somewhat like Rita Hayworth, determinedly exits the elevator toward Lallie's apartment. Tarly followed Boss here earlier and waited to decompress awhile before she entered the building. Lucky for her, Doorman left as well. Inside the apartment (The Sessameanys are now white-knuckling it even though they know the outcome. Everyone knows the story), she finds Lallie dead in the tub. Her work has already been done for her. She reaches into her bag, and deep into her butcher-past, and removes a Shun knife and expertly removes Lallie's head from her torso, and places it on her pillow. When Tig returns from the Dunphy's bar, he sees Lallie's door open, and gingerly enters and then rapidly exits. Berde, spying most of the night's action, thinks: *My, that Lallie's a sociable girl.*

Lallie's head resting on the pillow, as the TV screen flickers, and Sheldon enjoys the curried chicken in the kitchen.

Ex extracts the tattered page that was part of his old journal from his pocket. He holds it close to his person, 24/7, so he doesn't ever forget.

> "I try to run. I try to fight it.
> I push it away, but I'm ignited.
> It pulls me in, and I'm delighted
> to be in that zone where I'm beside it.
> And the pain is gone.

> "The push and the pull, battle within.
> Retreat and the lure. Virtue and sin.
> The struggle goes on. There's no way to win.
> The push and the pull. Virtue and the sin.

> "I try to breathe. I try to end it.
> I prod it away, it stays uninvited.
> It draws me back, and I am excited
> to be in that haze where life's unrequited.
> And the pain is gone.

> "The swallow of pills. The prick in the arm.
> The fade of all ills. The shadow of harm.
> The slow fade away. The deep drowsy calm.
> The push and the pull. The prayer and the psalm.

> "The push and the pull, battle within.
> Retreat and the lure. Virtue and sin.
> The struggle goes on. There's no way to win.
> The push and the pull. Virtue and the sin.

> "I try to run. I try to fight it.
> I push it away, but I'm ignited.
> It pulls me in, and I'm delighted
> to be in that zone where I'm beside it.
> And the pain is gone."

Hearty applause.

"Hello, I'm Jessie. And I'm an addict."

"Hi, Jessie."

"I'm celebrating one year and eight months of sobriety, 688 days to be exact." The group of 15 applaud again.

"Congratulations, Jessie. That's a great achievement. I know you've worked hard to get here, and we haven't seen you for a while; actually, since you got sober. Do you want to remind everyone about your story?"

"Sure. Seven years ago, I had surgery. Appendicitis. It was really minor, but this was before laparoscopy, and when they cut into me, they hit a nerve. I was in agony. My son, Garrett, was born a week after my surgery and I needed to step-up because my wife had serious complications with his birth, so I got a prescription for Percocet for pain. It was such an innocent act. At first, I hated the pill. It made me nauseous, but it dulled the pain. I started with one pill every few days, within a couple of months it was 12 pills a day. I was addicted. Soon, even the 12 wasn't enough. I moved on to Oxy, and eventually heroin. I learned how to shoot up from a YouTube video. By then, I was two years into addiction, and my wife left me, married another guy and banned me from seeing Garrett. It only made things worse for me, and the vicious cycle continued for a few more years. I worked hard to finally get sober. You all know how difficult it is. But I have great motivation. I'm fighting for my son. I'm sober and I want a relationship with my son."

After the meeting, Ex and the others mingle for a while. His story is so similar to theirs.

Pain. Doctors. Prescriptions. Life out of control, like a punctured balloon sputtering in the air. Linda was turned on by her boyfriend: "Try it. It'll make you feel happier." Abel's bulging disc is to blame. For Sofia it was a knee injury at 14, during a school soccer game. Down on the field, then down with opioids for 10 years. Lou had stage-4 cancer. It was chemo that gave him arthritic pain, not the cancer. Tina, painful periods. Midol, codeine, junk. Physical therapy wasn't doing the trick for Laura's tennis elbow and three years into the pain she purposefully crashed her car into the brick facade of her local Applebee's, so she could get more Vicodin than she was currently being prescribed. They talk over donuts, chips, coffee.

Sponsor reminds Ex that he'll be out of town for the sun-filled weekend and hands him a note with his emergency contact numbers on it.

"Don't do anything crazy while I'm gone."

SPIRIT

"It might be in the music, I say.
It might be in my heart some day.
And when that's true,
I know that you
Will be moved by the spirit too.

"There's a spirit that moves me.
There's a spirit that shines.
There's a spirit that moves me.
That moves me through time.

"It may be the truth.
It might just be the light.
But there's a spirit that moves me tonight.

"Sometimes things are so clear, you know.
If it's in you, somewhere it will show.
And when that's true,
I know that you
Will see how easy it flows.

"There's a spirit that moves me.
There's a spirit that shines.
There's a spirit that moves me.
That moves me through time.

"It may be the truth.
It might just be the light.
But there's a spirit that moves me tonight."

Yes, that's Matty Lynn's new hit record. The demand was so
great to follow up the blockbuster "Castaway," she sat down at
Toddy's trusty Yamaha and, as before, plugged away,
eking out a song once again inspired by her secret, unspeakable
muse.

"There's A Spirit" resoundingly proved she was no one-hit wonder. Demand was so great for her, Matty Lynn began touring again, even though she was not feeling her best. But she had the most devoted fans. Lady Gaga has her Little Monsters. Justin Bieber, his Beliebers. Barry Manilow, Fanilows. And, of course, there are the Deadheads. Matty Lynn has her Castaways. And she was just unable to disappoint them. Even to her physical detriment. Their spirit moved her. Just like other past spirits.

Berde, as vital in her 90s as she was decades ago, always felt a spirit was shadowing her. First, she thought it was her dear long-ago departed father, then her mother, then sweet Charles, to whom she was married for 60 years, and then Admiral Jackson. She always sensed a "presence" ever since Lallie was murdered, but never dared speak about it, lest someone might think she was heading toward dementia. She never even told Nettie, even when Nettie would get the shivers in Berde's apartment and say, "There's something very creepy in this building."

"Of course, there is," Berde would respond, "Someone was killed next door."

Nettie didn't like to visit there much, so Berde would go to Nettie's for cards or lunch, which wasn't so convenient, considering that Nettie lived in Kew Gardens, Queens. To make communication even tougher between them, Nettie has a phone that only allows her 688 minutes monthly, most of which is taken up by calls to her grandchildren.

Berde's feeling of a presence disappeared after the fire. Sure, five years change everything, but even the sky seemed brighter now, the air clearer. Trouble left their doorstep a long while ago. Until tonight.

The man who held the door for her, there was something about him. Perhaps it was the hoodie concealing his face. Or the desperate way he hunched over when walking. Head bowed.

He seemed mysterious, desperate and maybe even dangerous.

A car was parked across the street at Tomato, the restaurant formerly known as Spuds,
with its radio blasting "There's a Spirit."

There *was* a spirit guiding her to get back to her building and make sure all was right with her world. Big Theresa certainly kept guard during the day, but at night, lately, she's been getting into the habit of falling asleep right after dinner and her DVR'd *Wheel of Fortune*. Big Theresa was starting to lose her memory, so she was able to enjoy these reruns even though she's seen most of them twice. But after *Wheel*, it was off to bed for Big Theresa and Marcellus, and it was Berde's job to keep watch.

As she exited the elevator, she saw a stealthy figure quietly and deliberately close 688's door behind him. Princess Meghan barked at the figure, perhaps alerting someone inside that they were being visited by a shadowy silhouette.

Berde didn't know John was away and Sally was home alone with Garrett.

A chill ran through her body, reminding her of the night Lallie was murdered.

Lallie's death five years ago changed many lives.

Yolande, for one.

Upon quitting her maid's job where she worked for Boss and Tarly for a dozen years, she conscientiously earned her bachelor's at Farmingdale State College, not too far from Roslyn, Long Island, where she then lived in an airy four-bedroom apartment in newly constructed public housing with her husband Tomothy and four children.

During her early tenure at Boss's, Yolande spent her off-hours attaining her GED, taking night courses toward that college degree. It was a long, tedious process, sometimes registering for only one course per semester. When she quit Boss and returned to school fulltime, financial aid covered much of the tuition and she was awarded several scholarships which helped mitigate her growing student debt. After all, she had four children who'd be applying to college soon, and money was tight. Over the past years since the murder changed so many lives, Yolande completed her degree, earned a bachelor's in business, and was given full financial aid for Long Island University's MBA program at C.W Post College, about nine miles from Boss's former Sands Point home, and three miles from her current three-story colonial in a gated community in Roslyn Estates.

During those college years, Britt mentored Yolande, hiring her at Harbinger as soon as Britt took over the company when Boss was imprisoned. Yolande worked her way up to office manager, running the day-to-day operations of the bustling office. This was "a piece of cake," she'd joke when comparing it to running Boss and Tarly's chaotic household. With her bountiful salary at Harbinger's and continued support of Britt, Yolande's children's college funds are now secure.

Yolande thrived in the academic world, as she's now prospering in the business world.

For her final course of school, Business Comprehensives 688, Yolande wrote her dissertation on "Minorities in the Marketplace: How the Traditionally Bypassed Immigrant Can Save the American Economy." The MBA committee called it the best dissertation they'd seen in years. "Yes, Miss Tarly, your sapphire necklace is in the Lavender Suite." "Yes, Boss I'll clean your dog's poop." Maids.

While Yolande earned her advanced degree and climbed the corporate ladder at Harbinger, Tarly was in Bedford Hills Correctional Facility in upstate New York, a maximum security prison known for its infamous inmates including Amy Fisher, the Long Island Lolita who cold bloodedly shot her lover's wife in the face; Pam Smart, the young teacher who cold-bloodedly hired a hitman to kill her husband; and Jean Harris, who cold-bloodedly murdered her lover Dr. Tarnower, the famed author of *The Scarsdale Diet*.

Bedford Hills is snuggled in one of the wealthiest communities on in the country, and it's ironic that cold-blooded Tarly is among her people, and yet she's so isolated from them. It didn't matter where she was incarcerated, anyway. No one visits her. Not her kids who live an hour away, or her siblings who could take a quick flight from any of their homesteads. No calls, no mail. Well, some mail. Sandra, the former office manager of Harbinger, who was fired after the banquet-film fiasco, mails Tarly every news item she finds about the annual Met Gala, which drives Tarly into a rage. Each year, this vengeful gift from "Stupid Sandra," who Tarly wouldn't otherwise remember, the young woman who worked tirelessly, slavishly 70 hours a week for Tarly and her husband. The Met Gala would remain the bane of Tarly's existence. (The event Britt's attending in Christian Siriani.)

Never really feeling more than the Butcher's Daughter, despite her wealth and clout.

"Guard," she calls out. "I want to take a shower." No response.

Tomothy is planning a surprise for his and Yolande's 23rd wedding anniversary. He's remodeling their master bedroom's bathroom into a breathtaking spa for his beloved.

Tarly calls again, "Guard, I need to take a shower." Catty responses from other cells reverberate around her.

Tarly, serving 30 years, while her maid, and one of the many reasons she's in prison, is building a life to be proud of. And getting her own in-home spa.

"No showers today, inmate," a guard calls back.

PRODIGY

You can see the steam rise from the city streets, it's that hot.

Directly overhead, the sun is shining so brightly little Jenny stands stiff, immobilized for a minute. She attempts to get her bearings after spending three hours in rehearsal in Carnegie Hall's frigid air-conditioned Stern Auditorium with its muted lights that Jenny finds so conducive to practicing difficult classical pieces. Next week is her second solo appearance at the venerable musical venue, but it is her first in Stern Auditorium, the hall's largest performance space with its 2,804 capacity. Her previous appearance, two months prior, was in Carnegie Hall's medium-sized space, Zankel Hall, where she sold out the 599 seats and 89 SRO tickets. The sound of 688 people bellowing "Bravo!!! Bravo!!!!" each of the two-night event was heady. Well, for Tara at least, being the proud mom. For Jenny, she was just doing what she loved, and what she was good at. Stern's for two nights was certainly a big deal and was placing this talented tot in an elite group of artists. When Stern's two nights sold out, Tara was ecstatic, and she thought Jenny would be too. With her musical precociousness and general mature-for-her-age demeanor, it's easy to forget that she's just a kid.

"Are you OK?" Tara asks her daughter, while fumbling for her sunglasses in her Balenciaga pocketbook.

"Here, put these on," Britt suggests, as she hands the 5-year-old a pair of her heart-shaped sunglasses. Jenny smiles, a big toothless grin, because she loves everything about her half-sister Britt, and to wear her cool glasses? Well. That's everything.

"Mom. I don't want to do this anymore."

Tara, not catching on. "What, honey? What don't you want to do?"

"I don't want to play these concerts anymore," she whimpers.

"But you love playing the piano," Tara assures her, bending down so that they're eye-to-eye.

"And you're so good at it," Britt adds.

"I do love playing, I do, but I want to play when I want. I don't want to do concerts."

"But wasn't it fun when you did your first concert here?" she turns and points to iconic

Carnegie Hall.

"Yes," Jenny says.

"And wasn't that fun when Matty Lynn called you up on stage at her concert, and you got to play with her and Kelly Clarkson?"

"Yeah, that was lots of fun," she says now with a spot more energy.

"And when you were on *Jimmy Fallon*?"

"Yeah that was great," Jenny admits, but her decision to quit wasn't rash.

"So, what is it honey, what don't you want to do?"

"I don't want to play concerts. I want to play with Britt or be a teacher or put parties together, like Aunt Kara did."

"Well, Aunt Kara stopped because it turned out not to be fun anymore." Kara is now
Tara's personal assistant.

"You can do whatever you want," Tara says. "But you have a contract for a show next week. You have to live up to your contracts."

"Oh, noooo," she cries out. "Madison and Maddison told me Daddy's in jail because of bad contracts. I don't want to end up in jail too."

Tara and Britt exchange glances. If someone observed them on the street, they would take them for twins, not stepmother and stepdaughter, and most likely think the three were sisters, rather than two generations of a really messed-up family unit.

Britt, who is often eye-rolling when it comes to her kid sister, Madison, laughs it off.

"Oh, don't worry about what those two say. They are just teenagers."

Jenny takes whatever Britt says as gospel.

"Just do this one last concert," pleads Tara, "and then you can do and be whatever you want."

Taking everyone aback, she asks, "Can I be a guard in Daddy's jail so I can make sure he never gets out?"

"Uh, sweetie, I'm not sure that can happen."

"And then when he dies, I want to make a party like Aunt Kara did."

Britt turns to Tara, while Jenny's preoccupied adjusting her heart-shaped sunglasses, and cups Tara's ear, while whispering, "Yep. When he dies, that'll be some party."

Bath finished. Storytime over. Lights out. Time to go to sleep. Sally kisses Garrett goodnight, as John waves to him on FaceTime, in his fighting trunks, in the ring, before showtime in Chicago.

"Good night, Daddy," Garrett, says.

"Sweet dreams, little guy," John responds. "I love you."

"I love you, too, Daddy."

Sally kisses Garrett on the forehead and tucks him in one last time. She shuts his light, leaves the room and Day-Glo constellations shine brightly on his ceiling.

Garrett has an imaginary friend. Invisible. He's hoping his friend shows up tonight. He's sad that his Daddy's away and it would be nice to have someone to talk to other than his Mommy, who he knows is also sad because Daddy's far away at work.

His friend doesn't show up every night. Only sometimes. Not tonight, it seems. He lies in bed, Batman comforter and sheets up to his neck, waiting for Invisible, or sleep, whichever comes first. *No visitor tonight*, he thinks.

However, Mommy's friend is standing across the street from their building waiting for an opportunity to get inside. According to his research, it should be expected around 10:15. Ex finds that opportunity on time when the new doorman takes a quick bathroom break and Berde is leaving the building to walk Princess Meghan. He's surveilled this routine for weeks. He sees the doorman start to leave his post and as he crosses the street toward the building, he spies Berde walking toward the door from the elevator. Right on schedule. The predictability of humankind makes him laugh out loud. Ex holds the door for Berde and she thanks him, thinking, *This guy's trouble*. He takes the elevator up to the sixth floor and waits in the stairwell while he thinks. He knows John is out of town. He knows his schedule minute-by-minute. He knows when Garrett's bedtime is. He has become an expert on the Sessameanys.

Garrett's just about to doze and still no Invisible tonight. This apartment seems to invite invisibility. Ghost maintained a year-long residency here invisible to all, even her two best friends, Matty Lynn and Doctor, the only two people with whom she made contact. Neither Matty Lynn nor Doctor ever shared, with anyone, their encounters with Ghost, although they did share their experiences with each other, in great detail. They never told the police. They never told Toddy when interviewed for his film. Since the fire, invisible Ghost was gone, and now Invisible shows up befriending a perky little 7-year-old.

Garrett's quite sure his friend is a ghost, and although the grownups kept the details of the brutal murder from him, the story was so big that he was bound to get the details somewhere. He got information from everywhere. Garrett thinks his Invisible is Lallie. He mentioned it to his parents, and they told him about their own invisible childhood friends.

"All kids have invisible friends," they assured him. Mommy had Rosie, a girl her age with green hair and magical powers that enabled her to fly, and Daddy had Captain Powerful, a superhero who was so strong, he could bend concrete.

Right now, however, Garrett's so busy trying to communicate with Invisible that he doesn't hear Marcellus barking down the hall, alarmed by the man trying to pry open Garrett's apartment door. Big Theresa, after a long day gossiping under the blistering sun, in the park, was in a deep, dead-sleep, while Marcellus' yelps went unheeded.

Invisible materializes. In its own unseeable way.

It tells Garrett, "Trouble's coming."

Garrett, interrupted from the earliest stage of sleep, the twilight, thinks he hears "trombone's coming."

"What?" he asks, rubbing his eyes.

Invisible repeats, "trouble's coming," which Garrett hears quite clearly. This frightens Garrett and he calls out for his mother. Sally comes running in, turns on the light and comforts him.

"Our invisible friends are in our heads," she says. "We make them up. We control their actions. Maybe you feel guilty for sneaking those cookies I saw you take from the fridge today."

They laugh it out.

Meanwhile, Ex is in the living room waiting for Sally's return.

WILL

The will came as a shock. Still reeling from her sudden,
unexpected death, the last thing Matty Lynn's friends and family
were thinking about was her money. In life, Matty Lynn was
generous with the fortune from her music career. Not one
acquaintance was left wanting. They didn't even know about the
stolen money sitting in the bank, exponentially getting larger from
interest.

Toddy had already made his final amends with his best friend in
the hospital the night before she died. As with Matty Lynn's other
friends and family, Toddy was shocked by her turnaround. After five
years in remission, Matty Lynn's dying, a day after her heart attack.

"I love you, Toddy," she whispers weakly. "I have no worries
about you. You'll continue to prosper even more than now, if that's
even possible." She laughs. Her last.

Toddy is A-list. His James Bond outing starring Stuart as Double-
0 was a blockbuster, breaking all attendance records and wildly
reviving the brand. He has more top-shelf movie offers than Agent
can handle, and he is earning more money than he ever imagined.
Certainly, more than he dreamed of as a hungry videographer at
Harbinger.

"I want you to be my executor," Matty Lynn asks him, as he
keeps vigil at her bedside.

"Sure," he says, and jokes, "Do I get paid?"

"Not only don't you get paid, but I'm not leaving you anything."
She reaches for his hand.

"Sheesh, thanks," he mocks; he couldn't care less about an
inheritance.

"Seriously."

"OK, so who gets your vast fortune?"

Outside her door, they repeatedly page a Dr. Haleif. Over and
over again. Code red. Code Blue. Code Black. Haleif is missing
something big. Toddy sees that Matty Lynn is cold. The palliative
care room is cozy and hospitable, but it's freezing one moment and
stifling hot the next. His sweatshirt on. Off. On. Off. Toddy retrieves
a blanket from the closet and places it over the two that Tara, Kara
and Jenny had placed on Matty Lynn when they visited earlier this

morning; seeing her goddaughter, Jenny, brought welcome youth and innocent joy to this death scene. Toddy knows Matty Lynn is fading. Just last week she seemed full of life. In fact, the last five years since she got her "cancer-free" pronouncement she's been as energetic and vivacious as he ever saw her. That's why this setback is such a shock. Not yet 40, Matty Lynn's fading away.

Matty Lynn explains her will. "My money's going to the Lost Children, and I hope you'll appreciate it. All my other friends and family are doing just fine."

"You're an angel, Matty."

"Not quite yet," she responds, eyelids fluttering with fatigue.

Toddy leaves her with the laptop open to a group photo of all her loved ones taken five years ago at an impromptu remission celebration party held at Viva, which is still thriving.

Toddy kisses her goodbye, not sure if this will be the last time, and coos, "I love you, Matts. You mean the world to me. I'll see you tomorrow."

"Hope so," Matty replies, barely getting the words out, but she summons the strength to say her final words to him. "Love, you, too."

Alone, she adjusts the screen to better focus the photo, and a message comes through: "Love you, ML. Always have. Miss you. See you at 688."

She passes quietly into her new journey, as a legion of her Castaways keeping vigil ten stories below sing "There's a Spirit," not realizing she was now, indeed, just that.

Matty Lynn might or might not have read Lallie's ten-years-tardy message.

The earth quakes, the hospital shudders, the lights black out for one moment, as the ceilings weep tears from the pipes shattered in the moment. Ghost's way of crying,

"nooooooooooooooooo!"

****

All her friends and family gather to celebrate Matty Lynn.

Attorney, officious and brusque is there for one purpose—to read the will.

"Blah blah sound mind blah blah I love you all blah blah I leave my entire inheritance to Families United blah blah $37 million blah blah…

Wha?

Lallie thinks, *God bless interest and royalties.*

WRETCHED RAY

After her all-night discussion with 20-month-sober Ex, Sally felt secure enough to allow Garrett back in his life; even if he did break into her apartment uninvited.

A year later, she and John moved to San Francisco, sharing Garrett's custody with Ex.

And Wretched Ray and Laura moved into 688.

The apartment had gone through so many renovations it is unrecognizable from when Lallie lived, and died, there years ago. The parade of its residents was rapid in its turnover.

The aged building still sighs and strains, but the familiar faces of the past are not even memories to the new tenants. Morbid truths and urban legends that were the building's signature aren't a glancing notion to the current inhabitants. Without Berde and Big Theresa passing on their gossipy oral histories, there is no thread left to the past. Berde and Big Theresa are both gone. Gone-gone. Their cherished dogs, Princess Meghan and Marcellus? Recently dead and long-dead, respectively.

Little Theresa moved out, joining the Sessameanys in San Francisco, where John and Sally eventually had a daughter, Renee. Garrett decided to remain in Manhattan with Ex. He visits The City By The Bay during school breaks.

Mrs. LaRosa resides at the Sisters of Peace Nursing Facility in Staten Island.

Of the old crowd, only Invisible remains.

Wretched Ray owns the bar, Wretched Ray's, across the street from his apartment. He bought Spuds/Tomato five years ago, after losing his job with Todd Luft's Extreme Circus, which featured cringe-inducing sideshow acts. Wretched Ray made his living ingesting shattered-glass and razors. A piercer, he inserted nails, studs, rods, rings, knives and swords through various body parts, hanging weights on them/through them, delighting sadistic audiences. Laura, who he met on the job, was the alluring Circus Queen, a renowned sword swallower. She had Wretched Ray at "sword swallower."

Wretched Ray was fired for attacking Tubes, a circus-mate known for inserting three feet of plastic tubing into his body each night, and not by swallowing. Tubes made a foolish drunken pass at Laura, to whom Wretched Ray was then married. Wretched Ray crunched a beer bottle he was holding and then unceremoniously smashed Tube's face into a pulp with the crushed glass. Danger always followed Wretched Ray, but this was Todd Luft's final straw. The police were already looking for any reason to close down his traveling freak show.

Currently, Laura's life couldn't be more opposite than when she was Circus Queen. Laura is now a shut-in, although not of her own volition. Wretched Ray doesn't allow her to go out on her own, and doesn't think Wretched Ray's, an establishment for the area's tough, no-nonsense lowlifes, a freak sideshow in itself, is the right atmosphere for her. So, she stays home.

It's a dreary, hot Sunday evening. Wretched Ray has the night off. The apartment's AC isn't working and the rattle of raucous patrons and revving of motorcycles outside Wretched Ray's is wafting through their open windows. Laura is sitting at the kitchen table. Staring.

Wretched Ray just wants a night of TV, his DVR'd tattoo-competition shows, and then sex. Laura wants no part of either. When the programs are over, Wretched Ray launches into a tirade about how women shouldn't be tattooing. Laura knows what is next.

She is hot, uncomfortable, and in no mood for Wretched Ray.

"No. Not tonight Ray," she meekly sputters. And with one broad smack across her head, Laura lies unconscious on the kitchen floor. Wretched Ray leaves her there, gets into bed and turns on the TV to watch an MMA marathon. John Sessameany. The night slips past him and he falls asleep before the first kick lands.

When Laura awakes hours later, she stumbles into the dark bedroom where the TV's blue flicker provides brief spurts of navigation toward the bed, where she hopes to sleep and recover from Wretched Ray's attack. She gingerly slips under the covers, afraid to wake her abusive husband.

In the azure light of the TV, Wretched Ray's head rests on his stained, damp pillow, and a drip, drip, drip could be heard from the tub, in the bathroom.

PART THREE

OTHERSIDE

GLORIA

Lugging her cello up West 49th Street to the Eugene O'Neill Theater, where she will sub for the cellist tonight, Gloria Friedman is anxious to find some quiet space to harbor herself while her apartment is being painted. She's been subbing on and off for years here and is friendly with the cast and crew, and the stage managers allow her to use their backstage office when she needs a place to hang during the day before the show if she's early or has an appointment nearby.

Today's such a day.

Gloria lives in Hoboken and there are times when her commute is untrustworthy in terms of gauging time, so she often needs that refuge when she's early. Some crew member even had a nameplate made for her which sits on one of the stage manager's desks, since she's there so often. She loves Broadway, and she's subbed for many shows: *Beautiful, Kinky Boots, Wicked* and *Folk City: The Musical* (her favorite).

It's 1:30 p.m. and she's really early. She has an early meeting down the street at 3, and an early 5 p.m. dinner-date with Xavier, her business partner, at Cielo's bar, at the Mayfair Hotel next door to the theater. A quick drink and rustic pasta dish. Perfect.

What really has her anxious to get to a desk where she can sit for a bit is her desire to get directly to the email that just popped up on her cell.

"You have a new DNA connection."

Ever since she submitted her spit, she's been anxiously awaiting notice of new-found relatives, and here was the first.

By the time she walks toward the stage door, the church bells from the Actors' Chapel at St. Malachy's Church, across the street from the theater, play their weekly Wednesday 1:45 p.m. Irving Berlin classic, "There's No Business Like Show Business." The tourists eat it up, and to this day it still gives her a thrill. Gloria is not performing in the matinee today, just the evening show; the one she hears her favorite actress Natalie Portman is attending.

Gloria greets Dimitri, the doorman, who guards the stage door. She thinks he's cute and would date him in a minute, but he's more interested in her other job: professional ghost hunter.

"Did you look it up?" Dimitri asks her.

Rushed (those DNA relatives await!), she answers abruptly, "Not yet. I'll do it today, promise," and she scoots downstairs. She has a superstition, as do most theater people, and hers is to jump up and touch the right ear of the donkey that's hanging upside down in the prop area, just past the shelves of bibles. She has a different ritual for each play, but for *Mormon*, it's the donkey.

A few of the crewmembers scuttle around backstage, and she says "Hi," as she walks into the stage manager's office, places her cello in the corner next to the storage room, and opens her laptop to 23 & Me. And there she discovers Erich Friedman, a third to fourth cousin, and someone completely new to her. Before she Googles him, something catches her eye in an item on her screen. Apparently today is the 15th anniversary of a gruesome decapitation murder of a young woman in her NYC apartment. Gloria clicks the link and reads about Lallie's death, and some of the weird incidents that surrounded the homicide.

"Ah, a documentary was made about it," Gloria stage whispers. She toggles between 23 & Me and a few old news reports about Lallie and her murder.

She wonders to herself, *there must be a ghost there, right?* She makes a mental note to bring it up with Xavier when they meet for drinks later. As she starts digging further, completely forgetting about Erich Friedman, her cell phone vibrates. It's the stage manager at the Helen Hayes Theater. They need a cellist immediately. There are 597 audience members and 91 cast and crew depending on her. She sighs, closes her laptop and heads to 44th street. As much as she wants to obsess over Lallie, she can't let those other 688 people down.

PYTHAGORAS

Twenty years after Lallie's death, her building's gone co-op.

Residents are now owners, but Harbinger still manages it, and they're very careful to keep the building's past secret.

They've even renamed the apartments, assigning them only letters.

Floor one, "O"; second floor, "S"; third floor, "T,"; fourth, "F,"; fifth, "FI" and the sixth floor, "SI". Then the cardinal direction: N-S-E-W, ending with letters "A" through "Z" and then doubling up for the last four. Lallie's apartment, now owned by Laura, Wretched Ray's widow, is "SI-E-GH." Bill's is "SI-E- IJ." All this complication just to avoid that number.

With numbers eradicated, Harbinger hopes that the more-than-coincidental amount of mishaps and deaths in and around 688, err, SI-E-GH, will be erased from the public's consciousness. The new dwellers, paying 875K for their two-bedroom apartments, will have none of that.

But numbers live. And as the number 688 has been described by numerologists and spiritualists, it represents "a story that must be told." So here goes.

Long after Toddy introduced the world to 688, only a few true-crime enthusiasts even remember Lallie's story. There are about 300 murders in New York a year. Twenty years have passed and approximately 4,500 unfortunates have been murdered. Shocking as Lallie's story was, 20 years is a long time, and as awful as it sounds, there have been more heinous murders than hers…if there's even a way to judge these things.

Gloria Friedman now resides in SI-E-EF, Berde's former apartment. Her research brought her here. After discovering her distant cousin, Erich Friedman, was the renowned math professor known for a mathematical principle, "Friedman Numbers," she knew her destiny, and moved.

A left-brained musician, Gloria has no interest in math, nor does she have any idea about what occurred inside her neighbor's apartment 20 years ago, other than from internet research and Toddy's documentary.

Now settled, secure as a part-time cellist and fulltime ghost hunter, she decided to take her recent inheritance (her wealthy parents died in a still-unsolved boating "accident" in Punta Minta, Mexico. Her brother, Carl, the only suspect) and splurge on this obviously haunted high-end building. She first consulted with a mystic who confirmed:"Numbers have power."

****

Here's a math lesson:

The number 688 is what's known as a "Friedman Number," and a "Vampire Friedman Number" at that.

A Friedman number is an integer, which is the result of a mathematical expression using all its own digits in combination with any of the four basic arithmetic operators ($+$, $-$, $\times$, $\div$), additive inverses, parentheses, and exponentiation.

For example, 347 is a Friedman number because $347 = 7^3 + 4$. There are only 13 numbers with three digits that are Friedman numbers, and 688 is one example of that rare breed.

Why? When there's a factoring of 688, it uses 688's digits: 8 multiplied by 86.

That's math. What about the spiritual power of numbers?

"Numbers rule all things." That's Pythagoras talking. And he would know. He loved his mathematics. Numbers had souls, he believed, and they were dark or light, male or female, good or evil.

In mythology and religion, numbers are revered, and are often regarded as sacred: You have Buddhist noble truths (4), Christian Trinity (3), Islamic heavens (7), candles on the menorah (9), and, of course, those Commandments (10). The Greeks had muses (9) and the Norsemen had worlds (9).

A vampire number can be written as the product of numbers that together contain the same digits as the number itself. There are only three 3-digit vampire numbers: 126, 153, and 688. In this case, 688 is the vampire number, and 8 and 86 are what's known in those wacky mathematical circles as its fangs.

Like a vampire, 688, fangs in place, sucks the energy from others, while something else ultimately thrives.

Those who follow the spiritual meaning of numbers believe that "6" represents home life and "8" represents infinity. The double power of the two 8s, now amplified, means the overabundance of infinity…eternity. To numerologists, besides home and eternity, 688 is strongly tied to karma.

Some religious spiritualists believe that 688 is the Eternal Kingdom.

It is for Lallie.

Tig can't find his phone.

It's the damnedest thing. The same thing happened to him years ago back in New York City, around the time he first met Doctor. He's gone through four phones in the last month.

Tig's practice is thriving. Many people need therapy up here in Sleepy Valley, or Pleasant Valley, or Hamlet Valley, or whatever valley it's called. Ever since Dreamland burned to the ground, he and Doctor have returned to their professional callings and are living the high life.

"Hon, have you seen my phone?"

"Are you kidding me?" Doctor complains. "Noooo."

Pete, Tig's mirror image, pipes in, "Maybe you need to see a neurologist, Dad."

"Maybe you need to mind your own business," Tig says, slapping Pete on the head with the *News Beacon*. The family is enjoying a pleasant valley Sunday breakfast in their spacious yard. Tanya, 8, is playing in the pool with some school friends.

Pete pulls his lanky body up from the high-backed chair, and asks Tig, "Ya wanna play some tennis? Or are you afraid of getting beaten again?"

"Hey, I let your 12-year-old ass win last time." Doctor and Pete laugh, as Doctor reminds her husband, "Language."

Tig, still in good shape for middle age, jolts out of his chair, leaving his plate clean except for a wisp of maple syrup and a small, chunky piece of fatty bacon.

"OK, punk, let's play," he says, as Pete walks to the shed by the side of the patio to get racquets and a can of balls.

"Can you can find the court?" Doctor jokes, enjoying her dig.

Pete thinks it's the funniest thing he's ever heard.

They walk up the slight grassy incline to the court as yelps and girlish laughter waft from the pool echoing throughout the expansive estate.

Doctor sits back in her chair, fiddles with the last piece of waffle on her plate, decides against it, peels an orange and sits back to take in the scene. Life couldn't be any better.

Ringtone. It's Joni Mitchell's "Dreamland." Unlike Tig, she's had a more difficult time resolving what happened to her beloved club. The center of art and culture here in Happy Haven, Merry Meadow, whatever, was the most fulfilling part of her life. Sure, as a doctor she's saved lives, but that club was everything to her. It was a concoction of community and culture that was palpably human to her. And it died. A sad, lonely, tragic death. She wasn't even there to aid it or mourn it. She took it so much harder than Tig, maybe because she had a creeping feeling of how it really happened. A feeling she never expressed to anyone.

She looks at the number, doesn't recognize it or the attached name, and for some reason she decides to answer.

"Hello, is this Doctor Tate Senders?"

"Yes?"

"Sorry, you don't know me, my name is Gloria Friedman. I was wondering if you had a minute."

Doctor is watching Pete slaughter Tig on the court. *Hmm, he's damn good*, Doctor thinks.

Doctor's feeling generous today, "I do."

"Well, I live in your old building in New York City…"

A feeling of dread flushes her. For all the great times she had there (her first apartment; her friendship with Ghost, meeting Tig), she's spooked by the place.

"Hi? You there?"

"Yes, I'm here, Gloria."

"Could I meet with you and your husband to interview you for some research I'm conducting about the building."

"I'm afraid, Gloria…" Tanya is screaming, running from the pool. Her two friends are running behind her. Doctor tells Gloria, "Hold on, please," and throws the phone down, cracking the glass table and runs to the edge of the patio. Tig is racing toward the girls and herding them together with Pete, funneling them toward the house. Twenty feet behind is a brown bear.

"Oh, my god, get in the house, everyone!" Doctor picks up the phone and says, "Gloria, I'm having a bit of a crisis here. Can you call back?

"Sure," Gloria answers, adding, "I'm a ghost hunter and I'd like you to help me."

As close as they became, Gloria did not attend Boss's funeral.

Prison officials released a brief statement how Boss died, in the prison hospital, from an AIDS-related infection. Britt had been notified that he wasn't well, but that she wouldn't be able to visit him until he was released from the hospital unit.

However, Boss never made it out of the hospital unit, until it was in a body bag.

Gloria was devastated. She and Boss had become pen pals. She began writing him days after she first discovered the story about Lallie at her squatter's desk in the O'Neill Theater. They corresponded through eCorrections, a service allowing civilians and prisoners to exchange heavily censored emails. Surprisingly, he accepted her request and wrote back. He was alone in the world, shunned by fellow prisoners (except for a dispassionate sex partner or two), friends, former business associates and his family. Britt, Chase, Madison and Brenda from Buffalo decided to erase him from their lives forever. The stain and financial strain he left on his kids' lives was difficult to eradicate, and his inability to relate to them on an emotional level made the choice easy. Britt devoted many years to build the business up from nothing but shame. Gloria, not being family and being on a laser-focused mission, filled a void in his life: human interaction. He responded immediately to her introductory email.

"Hello. I hope you don't mind me contacting you. I'm Gloria Friedman, and I live in a Harbinger apartment. I'm a freelance writer [lie] and I'm curious about your life and work [Gloria knew how to manipulate men] and I was wondering if we could set up a line of communication where I can ask you some questions and you can respond. I'd love to know your whole story. Best regards, Gloria"

Boss: *"Send me your picture."*

Initially taken aback, Gloria seriously considered sending a photo of some Victoria Secret model, but she thought that someday they'd meet in person, and she didn't want to be discovered as a fraud. That's Boss's legacy. Deducing that Boss was a perv, starved for female company, she had Xavier take a sexy shot of her laughing at the busy bar at Viva, which survived almost two decades, thriving in commercially tenuous New York City.

Gloria sent the picture.

"Hello, Gloria. You've got pretty eyes. You look like Natalie Portman. Is that picture @ Viva? I haven't thought of that place in years. A different life. What do you need to know about me?"

"Hi! Everything. You're just so interesting. I hope you're doing well. Is there anything you need? Books? Coffee? Snacks?" Playing up to his ego was invigorating to Gloria. She didn't like Boss at all from what she could scope out about him online. She despised his womanizing and misogyny and was sickened by his corrupt and immoral business practices. But she needed to delicately work up to discussing Lallie. She knew it would take time.

"Send money. Then I can buy what I need in the dispensary. Also send more pics." So,

Xavier took another. At the beach. Gloria, in a skimpy bikini.

"Wow. You're hot. Do you want to visit?"

"Oh, I'd love to. Let's make arrangements. And thanks for the compliment. You're not so bad-looking yourself. Tell me, what was it like owning all that property? It must have been exhilarating. Was there a favorite property?" She needed to get him to talk about the apartment, which would eventually lead to Lallie.

"No. Buildings are buildings. Concrete, steel. How tall are you? How much do you weigh?" He's not taking the bait.

"I'm 5'6". I weigh 125. When can I come visit?"

"Whenever."

"How about Saturday, the 14th?"

"That's two weeks. Why so long?"

"I'm on deadline."

"What're you writing about?"

Gloria quickly checks out Google news. *"A 688-year-old skeleton just excavated in Brooklyn."*

"You make a living that way?"

She never told him about her lucrative ghost-hunting business.

Gloria visited. Often. He told her everything she needed to know about Lallie, the apartment and That Night. She fell in love. And then he died.

Toddy was excited. He never met a ghost hunter before.

"That's what you should do," Handsome says to Toddy, "You should remake *Ghostbusters* with an all-ghost cast."

Toddy knew his husband was kidding, but Toddy always thought out of the box.

"You know, let's see how this meeting goes. How cool would that be?"

Handsome laughs out loud. After all these years, Toddy never ceases to amaze him.

"Daddy, I want to see a ghost," Matthew chimes in." Are there kid ghosts?'

"I'll find out today, Matty, I'll ask the ghost hunter if she knows of a 6-year-old ghost you can hang out with." Matty runs to him and Toddy lifts him into the air. He's been on location in Greece for a month and he missed Matty so much he almost cancelled the shoot. Handsome, as usual, talked him down. "It will cost you a fortune. It'll bankrupt the whole film if you don't do this scene there."

"We can do it in LA, and then you and Matty can come on weekends."

"Toddy. The most pivotal scene takes place in the Pantheon. The actors are already there. And Streep has that prohibitive cancellation clause."

And so it was settled.

Toddy kisses the two goodbye and walks downstairs where Leonid, the most trusted chauffeur in New York, is waiting. He still works for Daveed, but he moonlights for Toddy when he's in town.

"Off to Hoboken, Sir?"

"Sounds like a good Bob Hope-Bing Crosby sequel, Leonid," Toddy chuckles. His spirits always rise when he's back home in New York with family and friends. Matty Lynn's death had him reeling for years, but adopting his beautiful son and naming Matthew for her has kept her memory alive in a vital, always-present way.

Leonid has no idea who Bob Hope or Bing Crosby are. *I can't keep up with these young new actors*, he thinks to himself.

Toddy is meeting Gloria at her old apartment in New Jersey, where Xavier and all her equipment resides. Gloria nervously prepares herself, practicing her pitch over and over again to Xavier whose eyes are beginning to droop from boredom.

"Stop worrying," he says, "You've got this."

"Toddy is an important key to my search. He knows this story inside and out."

"You're just geeking out because he's famous."

"Maybe," she laughs. Xavier retires to his bedroom.

Gloria rushes to the door when the bell chimes. She greets Toddy with a smile, and Toddy instinctively hugs her.

"Most important…did you br….?"

Laughing, Toddy, removes an Academy Award statue from his attaché case.

"Yes, Gloria, I brought it," and he hands it to her.

Gloria exults in its presence. Toddy rejoices in moments like this. He likes that his fame brings his acquaintances joy. And this new acquaintance seems like a keeper.

Toddy walks to the dining room where Gloria's cello rests on a stand.

"Wow, that's a gorgeous instrument," he remarks. "Would you play something?"

Gloria plays Camille Saint-Saens' "The Swan" and Toddy is transfixed, transformed. He is so moved he can't help but cry. The deep soul of the cello resonates throughout him. How a bow against strings can create such resonant perfection is beyond him. The hollow base just cries out, deep to his DNA. Toddy's director's imagination sets a rush of vivid scenes racing through his mind. He knows that the cello will drive his next film.

Gloria is thrilled to play this piece, retrieved from her distant memory. She's been so busy in "Oz" and "Uganda," that she has missed playing the classics. She sees how moved Toddy is and she's pleased there is a connection between them.

"That was just beautiful, Gloria," Toddy whispers, wiping his tears with his fingers.

Gloria reaches to the breakfast nook, and hands him a tissue. "Thanks, Toddy, I appreciate it."

"You are masterful. I definitely want to consult with you on the film I'm finishing off. Would you be interested?"

Surprised at the direction this meeting is taking, Gloria puts her palm to her heart and exclaims, "Yes. Yes."

They are besties.

"OK, Gloria tell me all about this ghost hunting business."

SHOES

Chase has big shoes to fill. Literally.

After Boss died, his will was probated. The feds took it all, billions worth of property and cash. His defrauded investors and financial institutions were repaid, with interest and penalties. And Tara already got her share. Boss retained $8 million in assets because prosecutors failed to ascertain that he obtained them illicitly. He squandered his remaining wealth rather than have his children profit from it.

Out of spite, Boss left the $8 million to Ruth Madoff. When Boss was imprisoned, thanks mostly to Stan's journal, Tara's craftiness and Yolande's resentment, Britt and Chase worked out a deal with the government to keep Harbinger. With most of the cash confiscated, they started from scratch.

He didn't shut the kids out completely. Britt got his $12,000 Salvatore Ferragamo Angiolo 2 alligator leather Oxfords. Madison was willed his $1,690 Tom Ford Gianni Lace-Up Cap-Toe (a very sleek looking shoe, she thought). And Chase inherited his father's $688 red Giuseppe Zanotti London Double-Zip Leather Low-Top Sneakers. Boss's will needed no mention of his young daughter, Jenny.

The kids never came to visit, ever, so the hell with them. His size 14 ½s were the statement:

You have big shoes to fill.

But the fact is they have been filled.

Boss's Ferragamos are now flowerpots in Britt's office for a beautiful, thriving pair of candelabra cacti. Madison donated her Tom Ford's to Everytown, a gun-control charity, to be farmed out to organizations that stage protests featuring empty pairs of shoes representing every lost soul for every community or school or house of worship or festival or Walmart or mall or concert or office or street or home, where there was a shooting. The issue hits close to home for her because high schools like hers have been popular targets. Chase, with his father's mind for making money, put the Zanottis up for auction on the same site that is selling Hitler's phonograph, Charles Manson's brown-fringed jacket, Ted Bundy's address book and Donald Trump's 40-foot red necktie, a prop he utilized to appear thinner. Boss's Brobdingnagian shoe size was no optical illusion. His feet were, truly, size 14 ½, which was extraordinary considering he was only 5'4".

Boss felt if he wore expensive shoes people would focus on his feet and not his short stature. It worked. If you asked someone how tall they thought Boss was they'd likely respond, "6'2"?"

Chase always knew his father was a little man, ethically. Privy to many of Boss's secrets, he despised him since childhood. Now, in his early 20s,, and years after the criminal case, Chase's suppositions proved true. As far as his mother? All the kids agree: Yolande was their mother.

Another trait Chase inherited from his father was his love of numbers. Money numbers. After Chase received his MBA, he told his twin, Britt, "I want to come onboard." She couldn't have been happier. She needed someone she trusted running the financial end of the business.

Chase happily and enthusiastically became Harbinger's CFO.

As CFO he's brought expansion to the company, like the addition of restaurants to the long list of interests Harbinger held: Harbinger Finance, Rentals, Hotels & (soon,) Restaurants. It took the then-17-year-old mind of Madison to suggest, "Just call it Harbinger FRHR." And so it was.

Chase is now happily married to Heir, inheritor of the Goodwin restaurant chain, owners of TokyoBar, Viva, both national Dumpling Heaven Bistro and Mangia chains and the enormously popular Sloppyburger with their cauliflower buns and super-juicy meatless patties.

Chase and Heir have a 2-year-old, Bethanie.

Madison and Maddison have been coupled since childhood. Considering the family Madison's from, her ability to remain an unexceptional, normal teen is what makes her remarkable. Maddison is an AMSR YouTube influencer who has made millions brushing her flawless face with feathers and eating potato chips into sensitive microphones. Jenny just graduated NYU.

"I'm married to Harbinger and my charities," Britt told the insatiable press, hungering for any progress concerning New York's most eligible bachelorette.

Britt married late, to Congressman.

Father: disgraced financial fraudster. Mother: decapitator of dead people.

The kids are alright.

"Are you ready to see what we do?" Gloria asks Toddy.

"Sure am," Toddy replies, with apparent glee. He has no idea what to expect, but he's in

for the ride.

Gloria takes him into the spare room, next to Xavier's bedroom, which serves as both an office and storage unit for their equipment. Toddy feels like he's on the set of *X Files*, or in the bedroom of a 10-year-old.

"Here we go," says Gloria, clearly as comfortable in this element as she was at the cello. "I'll show you some of the equipment and tell you what it does. If you have any questions, just cut me off." Toddy doesn't, for once she begins, he's speechless.

KINECT SLS CAMERA: "It works in pitch black," Gloria explains. "But the best part is it also works in full light. It can detect ghosts that you can't readily see with your naked eye."

SB7 Spirit Box: "This is one of my favorites. It transmits voices that aren't human sounds. Electronic voice phenomena, or EVPs, are unexplained voices that reach out to you when you are ghost hunting. They will give you clues that are personal or help you with your investigation."

Ghost Meter EMF Sensor: "Yikes, this was our first piece of equipment. It cost, like $35. We keep it as a memento."

ParaForce PMB Paranormal Music Box: "This is a really, really popular item. It's a music box that plays whether it's activated by a seen or unseen force. It's one of the hottest new pieces of equipment, and Xavier just bought it for our company's third-year anniversary. The music plays and then the light switches on. It is very cool, and an exciting piece of equipment for a ghost hunter to have in their arsenal."

Paranormal Thermometer: "It measures ambient heat, telling us when there's a spirit present."

Faraday Bag: "This is our Faraday Bag. It eliminates outside radio signals when using a Ghost Box, which is placed in the bag along with its speaker."

Radiating EM Antenna: "It's a pretty decent EMF detector, considering."

Ovilus: "The 5b is the most recent update of the Ovilus, which translates EVPS into the written word. Crazy. It has been very handy, because sometimes you can't fully understand the EVPs, and here it is documented for you. I like that it is impact-resistant because sometimes the ghosts are not happy with you and it can get a little wild."

ParaForce Ghost Box: "This is our Ghost Box; it has a built-in Faraday shield. It effectively blocks outside radio interference. I like that it has 12 different scanning speeds. Nice."

Wireless Headphones: "Of course, you need top-notch wireless headphones.

Paranologies Gyrascope Digital Talking Board: "This is how we communicate sometimes with the spirits. It's like a Ouija board on steroids."

Poletrcom Intelligent Instrument Transcommunication SpiritBox: "This is a popular item because it has a motorized sweep. And they are custom-made to your specific needs, so you can pick what kind of sensors and what speed you want."

Motion Detectors: "We have ultra-sensitive ones that pick up all EMF sounds and motion."

Spectracles: "Two HD cameras and infra-red illuminator and a super-sensitive microphone. To tell you the truth, there are a lot of goggles that are good. But I like the name. Ha."

PortalBlackOut: "This is the special edition. It is our latest and most expensive piece of equipment. It cost $688 but it is worth every penny. It's an amplifier *and* enhancer."

Watch: "You need multiple watches to document the time and confirm it with several sources."

Laser Grid: "It helps you make out shapes that are confusing to the human eye. It even helps determine mass. They're very cool, and very James Bond-y."

"And we always bring a First-Aid kit with us, 'cause, well, you never know.

"But even before you get involved with all the ghost-hunting equipment, you have to do your research. That's why I'm meeting with all you guys who knew Lallie and who had anything to do with that apartment."

Toddy, who thinks he's seen everything, is sold.

"Gloria, I want to go hunting with you."

"Hey Chief, how'd it go?" Leonid asks, as Toddy enters the car. Gloria is still on the street waving goodbye.

"Pretty interesting. I have to say," Toddy replies, still a bit disoriented. He and Oscar wave back. "Leonid, do you believe in ghosts?"

"No, Chief, I don't," he laughs. I have enough problems with live people."

After he drops Toddy home, Leonid drives to Queens to pick up Monica to bring her to JFK to pick up Angelica who will be visiting for a week, for Josefina's high school graduation. Geovany and Monica's other sisters are already in town. Daveed's in his study, closing a project he and Britt have been working on for two months. The phone rings.

The caller ID reads "Gloria Friedman." He knows Monica has two friends named Gloria; one from her book club and the other is a mother of a classmate of Josefina's that he knows only from back-to-school nights.

"Hello," he answers. "Hi, is this Daveed?"

"Yes, who's this?"

"This is Gloria Friedman. You don't know me, but I'm a friend of Toddy's. I'm a ghost hunter and…"

"Sorry, Gloria. It's a bad time to talk."

Daveed has no interest in ghosts. He's rushing to finish his work and then devote his weekend to family and friends arriving for Josefina's Saturday graduation, and then he and Monica are shuttling everyone to their beach house in East Hampton, which, fortunately, will comfortably accommodate his 50 sleepover guests.

As he finishes his report and sends it to Britt, a workman from his Hampton house calls to inform him that the pathway from the house to the beach is finished and will be perfect for use by Sunday. A stunning 57.3-foot boardwalk leading to the lapping waves of the Atlantic. All 688 inches of it bought and paid for by hard work and great pay. Life is good for Daveed. Why would he want to revisit Lallie?

Gloria checks Daveed off her list. She's disappointed about not meeting him, but more so that she wasn't getting to meet Josefina than whatever information Daveed would have been able to provide about the building and Lallie. She knew about Josefina, being the literal poster girl for immigrants' rights, well before she learned anything about Lallie's murder.

"Glor, the Epstors called. They feel lots of activity there tonight. Do you want to go, or should I bring Jackie?"

"Nah, Xavier, I'll go. I was hoping to interview Daveed, but he wasn't interested."

"Why? Did he say?"

"Yeah, it's his daughter's graduation, and he doesn't have the time. He was very nice about it, but it seemed to me that he just wanted to forget the whole experience. From what I've researched, he has enough ghosts of his own."

"OK, there are others. C'mon let's get our kits and go." Xavier is always helpful when Gloria gets down. He's a good friend. Jackie is lucky to have him.

The Epstors' house in Astoria is fabled in the neighborhood. It's been thought of as haunted for generations, and the former owners made a living from it, giving tours, having Estrella, a gypsy psychic, move into the basement to give public readings, and then there were their Halloween festivities, which raised thousands of dollars for charity. Now, the Epstors want nothing to do with it. They're kept up at night by thrill-seekers and bothered during the day by curious neighbors. They can't stand the rattling and the moaning in the walls, thanks to many "We don't know what that is, Ma'am," and "Ya got me, Sir," from contractors, plumbers and their local utilities. Their last resort is GloriX Ghost Hunters, Inc.

"Hi, Mrs. Epstor, how're you doing today," Gloria asks, as the haggard woman observes the equipment the two young hunters are carrying with them.

"Hi, Gloria, good to see you. Hello, Xavier."

"Hi, Mrs. Epstor, we're ready to get to work."

"Henry and I want to watch. Is that alright?"

"You need to be extremely quiet, though," Gloria warns, as she and Xavier put on their Spectracles and set up their trusty SpiritBox and new, expensive Portal BlackOut amplifier.

TÊTE-À-TÊTE

As with the other principals involved in Lallie's life, and death, Brother was initially resistant to Gloria's entreaties to meet. He eventually acquiesced to her unremitting pleas and agreed to meet her in Washington Square Park, a few blocks from his office on 5th Avenue, for a brief talk around lunchtime.

Life had gone on for him and Sister-in Law, and Kids and Car and Dog and Mortgage and Bedtime and Mornings and Work and Sheldon, who is now deceased (Arya, however, is happy to be spending her senior years with Toddy, Handsome and Matthew; bequeathed to Toddy after Matty Lynn's death.) Gloria could immediately tell that Brother retained way more of their flat-plain'ed Kansas upbringing than his sister, who from what she researched, blended in perfectly with the frenetic heartbeat of New York City.

"What do you want to know beyond what everyone already knows?" Brother asks. The heatwave has broken, and there's a brisk breeze mixing with the fountain's mist that is refreshing.

"That's just it. You're her sibling. You knew her the best and the longest. What one thing doesn't everyone know?"

"Probably that I know her the least of everyone. She never really liked me. I felt invisible to her. Or more to the point, she was the invisible one. She was never really present."

Gloria's intrigued. "Can you elaborate?"

"She was really never on the same plane as everyone else." Giving it deeper thought, Brother recalls, "Not even with herself."

"Gloria, it's hard to explain if you never knew her, but there was always something separate, spectral, about her."

The hair on Gloria's neck and arms stood erect, saluting the revelation.

Gloria looks confused.

"But lots of people liked her, I've heard," says Brother.

A folkie is singing Dylan's "Tangled Up in Blue" a few feet from them. A butterfly lands in his beard and he interrupts the song to swat it away. He isn't a very good singer, nasal and offkey, and his guitar playing is rudimentary, but a Swedish couple give him a dollar as he attempts to untangle the butterfly.

"Yeah, you'd like her if she liked you. If not, watch out. She could be relentless. Steadfast. Vengeful. Obsessive."

Gloria's curiosity is roused, "Tell me more about her 'otherness?'"

He continues, "Even her self-harm was symptomatic of that apartness she always possessed. It was like she was inflicting pain and injury on someone else."

"Was she schizophrenic?" Gloria asks. It's a question no one has expressed before.

Brother has a quick reply: "No. She was under the care of so many shrinks throughout her life, and not one of them thought that. They knew she was weird, but they never had a clinical name for it. You would be talking to her and she would just disappear. She was in another world for sure."

"I have a weird question for you, but did she believe in ghosts...in an afterlife?"

Brother laughs, deeply, "I think that might have been one of her obsessions." Gloria, who has been inching toward Brother more and more during their conversation, notices a slight scent of whiskey on his breath. She looks at her watch, it's only 1 p.m.

"Really?" she asks. "How so?"

Ever since she was a kid. She would love scary movies that had ghosts. Ghosts in mansions, ghosts in churches, ghosts in graveyards, but mostly she loved when ghosts used their powers to manipulate the physical world."

"Ha!" Gloria shouts.

"You know she had a tattoo of Casper on her forearm?"

"Casper? 'The friendly ghost'?"

"Yep. Him." Brother looks at his watch. "Well, it was nice meeting you, Gloria, but I gotta get back to work." He enjoyed his brief tête-à-tête with a woman other than Sister-in-Law, and a pretty woman at that. Gloria thinks, *No wonder she was invisible to him; she was such a life force and he is so utterly dull.*

Ugh, Mangled Up in Blue has restarted.

"Yeah, it was great to meet you as well. Thanks for all your information."

"Gloria? Do you think Lallie is a ghost?"

"If she is, I'll find her," Gloria says emphatically.

Nothing much came of the Epstors' ghost hunt. Lots of white noise and EVP activity, but nothing really specific. Xavier is getting weary of these fruitless hunts. While still a believer, he is just frustrated that a hobbled, old Civil War Captain who died of gout or an innocent beautiful young virgin pushed down the stairway haven't yet revealed themselves. Or discovering an orphan buried in a wall. Even a purr from an 18th century cat disposed of after using up all nine lives. Just a lot of static, ambient heat presence and movements so rapid they were barely perceptible. And some of that static could have been Ariana Grande on Z-100.

Anyway, Xavier is ready to move on. Jackie is itching to relocate to her hometown of Bangor, Maine, and Xavier feels the change will do him good as well. He'd leave the business to Gloria, who is way more into it than he is, and her interest only seems to be growing. He has no doubt that one day Gloria will make spirit contact. He'd regret not being there, but the lure of rural Maine, and Jackie's wishes is too appealing.

The Epstors are so excited about the static, they're beside themselves. Ghosts! In their house. Before GloriX Ghost Hunters arrived, they feared they might have ghosts; now they celebrate it. Experiencing the hunters in action, with beeps and swirls on their machinery, well, that was just about the most exciting thing they've ever done. And they were at Woodstock!

Hourly, they're even now consulting with Psychic Estrella, who's also captivated by the hunt.

Gloria's drained. She takes ghost hunting so seriously she needs to recover for days post-hunt. But she can't regroup today. She has an appointment with Agent and Stuart, and she hasn't slept at all since the appointment was made, daydreaming about meeting Stuart. He's her biggest celebrity crush.

Her appointment is at 2, so Gloria begins her beauty ritual at 10. Nothing can go wrong. Hair must be perfect. Make-up, stunning. Dress, a knockout. Shoes, as high-heeled and sexy as possible. To hell with her Morton's neuroma. She can tolerate the pain for one day. Shower. Shave. Prep. Car service (no way she was going to sweat it out in a subway or some seedy Uber or cab).

Stuart and Agent aren't essential to her research, but it's a sneaky way for her to get to meet Stuart, while still gathering some intel on Lallie. Stuart's at the height of his career. The Oscar did wonders for him. It allows him to pick and choose what movies he's going to star in, instead of wondering which movies will feed him.

The years treated them well. He and Agent have beautiful identical-twin girls: Mollybelle and Abigail. Of course, they're gorgeous. Look at their parents. At 6 years old, the girls are earning more money in commercials and modeling than Gloria in all of her ghost hunting. Their cute little mugs are ubiquitous—commercials, magazines, billboards. Mollybelle is the face of Verizon, and Abigail just won a Clio Award for her star turn in Subaru's "As If Their Lives Depend On It" commercial, which aired during last year's Super Bowl, overshadowing the white-knuckle, game-changing final play.

Agent, into her 50s and suffering from Lyme disease, is ready to retire. But not until she has secured her girls in TV and film, and that is currently in the works.

As Gloria is preparing, refreshing her make-up one more time, the TV rattles on in the background. Something about a white supremacist shooting up a mall in Alabama. The news doesn't break Gloria's stride. She's is becoming immune to these daily atrocities: Alabama, Mississippi, Texas, California, North Dakota, Minnesota, Nevada. Everyday another horror.

As she's about to leave, luxury car #688 parked outside her building, her ParaForce PMB Paranormal Music Box begins to play. It's a jolting and eerie sound. There's a life force near her closet. The one adjoining her neighbor in SI-E-GH, Lallie's old apartment. All primed and pretty, ready to meet Stuart (and Agent), Gloria now has a dilemma. Heartthrob or ghost hunt.

STARBUCKS

Bill's pacing in Starbucks. He walks to the napkins; picks up a
few. He wipes the sweat from his brow, neck and upper lip. His heart
is racing. He's successfully flushed Lallie's murdernight from his
memory, and this meeting with Gloria is revisiting it in a rush of
anxiety. His face feels flushed, so he asks Joy, the barista, for a cup
of ice. He puts two cubes in a napkin and massages his face with it.
He feels better.

A pretty woman, about 5'6'', with burnished brown hair and a
familiar look (Anne Hathaway? Kiera Knightley? Natalie Portman?)
walks up to him and asks, "Bill?" She extends her hand, and says,
"I'm Gloria." Bill thinks how much he'd like to photograph her.
He's always had a knack for finding uniqueness in the ordinary.
Great bone structure, he thinks, intently examining her.

"Gloria. Nice to meet you." Not in the least. He regrets accepting
this appointment.

Bill already has his drink, a venti chai latte. Gloria orders a
grande nitro cold brew with soy milk, and a cookie.

"That'll be six eighty-eight," Joy says with a toothy smile.

"Want to find a table?" Bill suggests, and they locate an isolated
booth by the restrooms and sit. Counting Crows are playing in the
background. She hates Counting Crows; she prefers the real deal,
Van Morrison. Her father used to call her his "brown-eyed girl."

"How're you doing?" she asks.

"I'm good," he answers, uncharacteristically jittery. He's known
for his dispassionate personality. Gloria doesn't believe him because
she can see the Nixon sweat, and the light behind her is glaringly
reflected on his damp forehead. And those inflamed rosy cheeks.

"Good to hear," she says.

"So, you're a ghost hunter? What does that entail exactly?"

"I go to haunted places and seek out the spirits that reside there. I
know it sounds far out, but once you get caught up in it, it easily
becomes an obsession."

"You think Lallie's place is haunted?"

"I'd like to find out." Gloria feels a pang of regret choosing Stuart
and Agent the other day, instead of further investigating what was
causing the Music Box to be so active.

"Well, I don't know how I can help you. I never noticed anything ghosty about her."

Gloria laughs. "Bill, while you were in New Mexico, after Lallie's death, did you ever experience anything supernatural?"

Bill breaks into a hearty laugh. "Gloria, I was in New Mexico."

Gloria appreciates his joke. "Seriously, I mean anything to do with Lallie. Did she ever come to you in dreams, or in some physical or spiritual way after her death?"

He replies straight-faced. "Hundreds of times."

"Can you give me an example?"

"I'd dream about her all the time. I hear her voice. I smell curry chicken, which was the last meal we had together. I'd see her on the street. I can go on."

"You think she's haunting you?" Gloria thinks she might have finally caught a live one, but Bill laughs it off.

"Hell, no. I think she's just stuck in my head." Gloria thinks it's more than that and she believes Bill probably thinks it's more than that, but she never pushes her agenda on anyone.

"Yeah, for sure. Why wouldn't she be?" she assures him.

Unconsciously wrapping her hair into a bun with her index and middle fingers, Gloria drifts. Bill likes her neck. *It would photograph beautifully,* he thinks. He'd also like to sleep with her. *Maybe if I lead her on a bit*, he wonders.

"Yeah, maybe she's haunting me," he lies.

Swirling a small straw in her nitro cold brew, Gloria, in her head, is back in her apartment. *I wonder what caused the Music Box to activate? I have to get into Lallie's apartment somehow. How?*

When she finally arrives home, with an appointment to meet Bill at his apartment Friday night, she rests on the couch; it was like pulling teeth. Her phone is vibrating, and it's a call from Agent. She and Toddy want to produce a reality show around her ghost hunting, with the pilot focusing on Lallie.

MAGNET

As he walks down the street, everyone takes a second look at Garrett. A confident stride, a simmering stare, and his striking similarity to some impossibly handsome movie star they just can't place isn't really all that draws their attention. There's something magnetic about this 22year-old, inexplicably drawing others to him. Humans appear ferromagnetic, and he's the draw. A nickel, an iron nail on the street imperceptibly creep to his feet if he were standing on the corner hailing a cab. Cobalt glazed pottery might fly off a shelf or tiles rise from rooftops when he passes. Why are so many people attracted to him? Perhaps it's the iron in their blood and cobalt manufacturing their B-12.

So, was Invisible real? Was there something corporal there or was Garrett suffering psychotic episodes because of the stress of his parents' vitriolic divorce. Now that he's older and his parents are amicable with each other, he's been without Invisible. But that's also because he no longer lives in SI-E-GH, Lallie's old apartment. At least that's Gloria's theory.

Gloria has spent, perhaps, more time with Garrett than anyone else involved in the apartment's history. She spoke with the Sessameanys, Little Theresa, and other tangential residents of the building, but no one sparked her interest more than Garrett Sessameany. Maybe it's that magnetic attraction, but she can't get enough of him. He's been gracious and candid, filling in many blanks for her. He doesn't mind talking about his past and is interested to see where Gloria is going with all this research. After his fruitless 15-year search for the truth, maybe it is Gloria who might provide the answers. Who or what is Invisible? Was that apartment a portal, where ghosts could come and go as they please? Before she died, Matty Lynn told Garrett about Ghost, but she swore him to secrecy. He hasn't even shared that information with Gloria, but he knew that she was intuitively developing the Lallie-as-ghost theory on her own.

A young woman, in her early 30s, trips over a grating as she passes Garrett on his way to his weekly meeting with Gloria. He caught her attention, and she lost her step. He walks over to her to help her up. The other passersby walk past her, but their gaits slow as they pass Garrett.

As he helps her up, she purposefully brushes her arm against his arm. She had to.

"My hero," he hears, as he resumes his walk toward Carmelio's in Gramercy Park. It's Gloria, and she's laughing. She's seen this tug of attraction before.

"Yes, I'm feeling heroic today."

"I don't know about you, but I could use a very tall, strong drink," Gloria says, and proceeds to tell him about her lack of progress with immovable Laura. Gloria wants access to that apartment, but Laura keeps putting her off, telling her to meet her at Wretched Ray's instead. Laura's no help. The former Circus Queen is frustrating her so much; *damn it, just let me in.*

Sitting at an intimate table for two at Carmelio's, Gloria catches a glimpse of a striking blonde and her companion speaking jovially with the maître d'. The blonde looks familiar, and Gloria nudges Garrett, asking him who she is. Garrett also thinks she looks familiar but can't place her either. The table for four next to them, filled only by two, erupts with activity as the duo wave wildly attempting to get the arriving blonde's attention.

One yells out, "Britt!"

The other, who must be her identical twin, continues waving and pointing to their table.

Britt smiles at the maître d' and points to the table and he walks her and her companion over.

"Damn, that's Britt," Gloria exclaims. "I've been trying to reach her for ages." Britt walks over to the table for four, hugs the two, and greets them: "Tara." "Kara."

"Damn, that's Tara," Gloria exclaims. "I've been trying to reach her for ages, too. Garrett thinks, *If money could wear a dress and heels, it would be Tara.* She just oozed wealth.

Britt, her companion and the twins chatter away.

Gloria starts plotting.

LEVITTOWN

Years after Det. Gerarra retired and suffered a curious stroke (he'd been perfectly healthy), he still likes to discuss his favorite case.

He is happy to welcome questions from any reporter and nosy neighbor, friend or family member. Wheelchair-bound, he has nothing but time on his hands and he still sees himself as the hero of the 688 case, despite the fact that he pretty much mangled the investigation and was upended by the likes of Toddy, a young, gay, amateur filmmaker.

Gerarra's house in Levittown, Long Island, looks like every other ranch on the block— the original Levitt homes—and like so many other houses in his neighborhood, Det. Gerarra's home proudly flies a black-and-white American flag with a blue horizontal line running through it, flying on a pole extending from his porch. The thin blue line. The police flag, in honor of fallen comrades. His proud profession.

Gerarra lives alone, so he always enjoys company. Valerie divorced him shortly after Lallic's murder; he just became impossible to live with, spending the majority of his time obsessing over the case. His kids are in Atlanta. Both cops.

Regine set the table for two. A bowl of fruit and a cheese dish. A few bottles of flavored seltzer are on the table, along with a small platter filled with fresh cold cuts from the deli, and potato salad. She's been his aide for three years, and for a fiercely independent guy, he's come to rely upon her heavily. He's considering asking her to move in and reside in the renovated den he converted for his oldest son, Tommy, a lifetime ago. His benefits would cover that.

Regine greets Gloria and walks her to the kitchen. Regine has already helped Det. Gerarra from his wheelchair into his favorite cushioned chair (different than the other three at the table), and Gloria bends to shake the detective's hand, while she thanks him for inviting her for lunch.

As Gloria explains her ghost-hunting work, Det. Gerarra's mind wanders. From what he's seen (friends' videos, her family's old home movies) of Lallie over the years, Gloria reminds him of her. Granted, Lallie had a secret, maybe Gloria does too. But his cop

Spideysense informs him that Gloria's a good egg (although, later, he tells Regine, "Gloria's a likeable nut job"), who he believes has a genuine interest in him and his story. Lunch turned to dinnertime, as Gloria rambled about EPVs and Det. Gerarra regurgitated everything he knew about Lallie and the apartment, with Gloria taking notes and recording his every word.

Regine broiled pork chops (Gloria hasn't had a homemade pork chop since she was living at home; probably around 16 years old). She savored every bite.

"This was delicious, Regine. Thank you so much."

"She's the best," Det. Gerarra says, with a weary smile. He's getting tired. It's been a long day. After dessert (vanilla ice cream) and coffee (decaf), Gloria leaves with lots of supporting information for her already extensive research. She made sure she expressed what a great job Gerarra had done on this investigation, although she knew it wasn't true. He knew it also. Regine, who has heard the story about 300 times, believes he *is* the hero of the story, because she has only heard Det. Gerarra's side of it. She thinks he's an investigative genius for figuring out it was a suicide. A suicide with a bizarre twist. Only a detective as smart as her Frank Gerarra could have figured that out.

Meanwhile, back home, Toddy, who *did* figure it out, is in his study, working on the pilot for Gloria's reality show that he'll be producing with Agent. He'd been ruminating over the idea ever since he met Gloria and when Stuart mentioned to him that they had met with her, it clicked.

Let's put on a show, kids.

Toddy's lost in the script he's composing longhand when he sees a message flash on his computer. He leans over, clicks on the new message, and all it reads is, "Please tell Gloria to keep trying to find me. Don't let her give up. I'm waiting."

Yolande's four children take turns visiting her in the nursing home. She's done well; money's no object in terms of her top-level care. She attended to Tomothy and their kids all those years, and now it's their time to care of her. They tried homecare nurses, but she needed too much medical attention. Alzheimer's is the scourge that snatched their mother from them. The siblings are scattered around the country, but they each regularly return to see her.

Be'Linda, now widowed from Yolande's brother, Yaro, helps Tomothy with Yolande's care. She lives near the high-end dementia-focused medical facility, and with her nurse's background, she's taken on the responsibility of daily weekday visits. Tomothy's there every day. Besides family and friends, Yolande's Harbinger colleagues also visit, but as she deteriorates, they come less and less, except for Britt and her siblings, Maddison and Daveed who visit weekly.

Physically sound, there's days when she's simply obstinate. She doesn't speak or react. Other days she'll be manic and rant about her childhood, in such detail it stuns her family. She's particularly worried about the war in Vietnam.

"I hate Nixon," she says, vehemently shaking her head. "I want Yaro home now!"

Then there's the times when she talks about Lallie. To put a finer point on it, she talks as if she *were* Lallie, describing details of Lallie's past that send chills down everyone's spines. She talks about Girlfriend and a barbell. She rails on about Little Theresa and her damned cat. Touchy feely Mr. La Rosa. Spuds. Muggers. Nasty workmen. Little boys who have secret friends. Tig's phones. Daveed's party. Nettie, Berde's friend…

"Why's she so scared of me?" Yolande asks. She'll query how Sheldon is.

"Who's Sheldon?" Be'Linda asks Tomothy. He just shrugs. His days are filled with shrugs.

Yolande speaks longingly of Doctor, and lovingly of Matty Lynn. And then she'll break out in maniacal laughter, crying out, "Oh, all that money we have."

And then she'll retreat to silence again. As if her soul left her body.

When Gloria heard about Yolande's situation, she was beside herself, and this turned out to be the longest negotiation of all. Finally, Tomothy relented, realizing that had Yolande been in her right mind she would have jumped at speaking with Gloria about her vital role in the convoluted murder mystery.

Without Xavier by her side, (he and Jackie did make it to Bangor), Garrett's now helping Gloria. When they arrive at Midwood Medical Residences with all their equipment in tow, Be'Linda is concerned that their appearance (strangers) and odd-looking instruments (Spectracles!) might frighten Yolande, who often was agitated about not knowing where she was.

"Am I going to kindergarten today?" she asked her children, Sis and Tomas, yesterday. So, while Gloria Friedman and Garrett Sessameany sign in, a vacant Yolande is being prepped for their entrance.

As soon as she sees them, Yolande brightens. She sits up straight, combs back her hair with her palm, shoots her right arm out in a stiff invitation to shake and says, "Garrett, so good to see you."

Everyone is taken aback. Yolande never met Garrett. Maybe it is that "attraction" thing he has going. Garrett takes her hand and suddenly jolts as if electrocuted. Yolande's hand shoots out once again, and while a bit leery, Garrett braves another shake, which she doesn't release, continuing to pump it.

"Good to see you, again," he responds.

Be'Linda glances toward Tomothy, and then to Garrett. "You know each other?"

"No," says Garrett.

"Oh, I thought you said, 'again'," Be'Linda asks.

The next four minutes is just Yolande's gibberish. However, Gloria's machines are recording a lot of EVP activity and she's concentrating more on monitoring them than deciphering Yolande's comments. That's until Yolande demands, "Laura must let you in."

"What? What was that, Yolande?" No response. Empty look; her body retreating.

At that moment, the Transcommunication Spit Box explodes in a cloud of smoke. With alarms blaring and personnel pouring in, it is almost inaudible when Yolande turns to Garrett, puts her hand to his head and whispers something.

"Did she just say 'trombones coming'?" asks Gloria.

GRADUATION PARTY

Josefina's party is off the hook.

New Orleans-themed in honor of Tulane, where Josefina will attend on full scholarship. The food catered by Chef Emeril Lagasse, a personal friend of Chase, who's successfully expanding Harbinger into the restaurant business. Jenny, Tara's daughter, now 20 and an aspiring event planner, is successfully overseeing the celebration. The Big Easy Brass Band is the entertainment.

Britt and Tara huddle discussing joint philanthropic interests. Tara never remarried after

Boss. She wanted to hold on to her money. Britt's 10-year-old daughter, Raven, is shadowing Jenny, her idol. They've been like sisters to each other since Raven's birth. Congressman, Britt's husband and Hannah's adoring father, is in D.C., at an all-night, secret emergency caucus.

Something bad's afoot.

Last week, Britt finally met Gloria and by the end of their spirited conversation, she thought it was a great idea to invite Gloria to the party. A few people involved with Lallie's case would be there, and she'd make a personal introduction to Daveed, even though she agreed that he probably wouldn't have much to offer Gloria toward her research.

"Please bring a date," Britt suggested.

"Thanks, I will," Gloria said, relieved. She wasn't a party girl. She'd bring Garrett.

When Garrett and Gloria enter, obviously, he generates much ogling. Especially from Josefina, who points to Garrett quizzically. *Who's that?* After extensive therapy, some speech has returned, but not by much. Jenny, master of reading her friend over the years, shrugs her shoulders, "No idea."

Bashful grin, Josefina waves her on. *Please find out?*

"For sure," Jenny laughs, and strolls over to introduce herself.

"Hi, I'm Jenny. I'm tonight's event planner." She's a striking blonde, just like her mom was when she was the young widow courted by Boss.

"Oh, Jenny, so nice to meet you, I'm Gloria. I was invited by Britt. This is Garrett."

"Nice to meet you both," Jenny says, unable to shift her glance from the most handsome young man she thought she'd ever encountered. Josefina and her friends stand huddled, gawking, fingers over their mouths waiting in anticipation.

"The party looks fantastic," Garrett says.

"Thanks. It took a lot of work."

"Well," Gloria remarks, as if Jenny were even paying any attention to her, "it is for a very special young woman."

"For sure," says Garrett.

"For sure," responds Jenny, flustered. She waves Josefina over.

"Gloria, Garrett, this is Josefina, tonight's star."

Gloria can't control gushing, "Josefina, it's an honor to meet you. I've followed your story from the start. You're quite a role model."

"Thanks," manages Josefina, blushing; from being in Garrett's company, not from the compliment.

Someone's tapping a champagne glass with a spoon, just as a wandering waiter offers the foursome champagne of their own.

"Josefina, please join us?"

As Josefina walks to the stage where Daveed, Monica, 15-year-old Daveed Jr., and Bingo2 await, the Big Easy Brass Band begins to play, NOLA parade style.

"Trombones coming," Gloria jokes to Garrett. He shudders, remembering something dark, indistinct. The band quiets as Daveed, gray at the temples, begins to speak.

"Congratulations, my beautiful, brilliant daughter. Out of 688 kids in her graduating class, she's valedictorian!" Weepily: "Especially after our incredible journey together…and apart…I'm so prou…"

There's sudden chaos, shouting. The party's being raided by ICE (recently elevated to a cabinet-level department). In fact, ICE is the reason Congressman was suddenly summoned to DC for an emergency session about raids that would be taking place nationwide.

Closer to home, Daveed is being rustled away by a gun-wielding agent. The 4-hour-old ICE-related executive order negated the grandfathered citizenship Angelica wrangled for him and he's now to be extradited to Guatemala, where he'd, no doubt, be executed by vindictive gangbangers. Waiters, bartenders, chauffeurs were also being rounded up in the frenzied scene. Britt and Tara, whose immigration-rights organizations are the nation's most powerful, don't waste any time making calls.

But it is Gloria, who inadvertently intervenes. Henry Epstor is the ICE agent herding Daveed and when he sees Gloria he is momentarily disoriented, long enough to allow Garrett to whisk Daveed away.

Josefina is thinking, *now it's my turn to save my dad.*

Bedford Correctional Facility is having technical difficulties.

Everything electrical is going awry, along with periodic blackouts. The mysterious source is proving difficult to discern. Alarms are going off, blaring randomly, for no apparent reason. The water sprinkler system has a mind of its own, showering prisoners and staff in unpredictable intervals. Security cameras shut down, and electrical locks and gates lose power. Emergency lights eerily flash on and off in darkened hallways. Tammy, Tarly's original cellmate, says the noisy, sensory-overloaded scene reminded her of when she and her boyfriend, Clifford Lee Simmons, went on a shooting spree in their high school, killing three and injuring 38. Clifford Lee, always a coward, shot himself dead.

The already short-fused inmates are on edge, and the administrators and guards are overwhelmed. Additional security is called in from local police forces to supplement the inundated staff. RoRo, Mitchie and Tarly are having none of this and decide, after almost 20 years of spotty behavior, they would take advantage of the situation and will attempt to escape. A plan they were plotting for years.

After decades of incarceration, Tarly, is now as hardened a criminal as any of her fellow inmates, especially RoRo and Mitchie. Her society days are far behind; the rearview mirror.

Maybe this is what the butcher's daughter was always destined for.

There's a hierarchy here at Bedford. Husband killers are the upper tier. Child killers, the lowest. But decapitating a dead person? Well, that never really happened before, so "firsts" were very highly regarded. Despite the extreme level of respect that commanded, Tarly did not have an easy initiation when she first arrived. She was used to being doted on and bossing others around. It took years to finally break her, seven, eight, but break her it did. She is now indistinguishable from any of her prison peers.

It's been a lonely existence. No visits from family; never had any friends. So, RoRo (murdered a night watchman in a bungled drug-fueled robbery) and Mitchie (murdered her longtime girlfriend who cheated on her) have become her go-tos. Incapable of meaningful emotion, Tarly developed a deeper connection with the murderous duo than ever with Boss. But being the social beast she was, she missed commonplace interaction, even if it was bossing around an underling, or sniping at a waitress.

Missing the civilian world, Tarly's flat emotional state perked up significantly when she received Gloria's letter, a rambling screed about how valuable a source she believed Tarly would be, considering Tarly experienced Lallie *post mortem*. Tarly was intrigued by Gloria's ghost hunting, because she could swear Lallie was haunting her, even though her rational self knew there was no way it could be true.

RoRo goes through the plans her ever-scheming mind has put into place within a half-hour of the prison blackout. She knows what exit will be accessible, unlocked and unalarmed. She figures how the three will get there and where they will go when they flee. Ordinarily, she would have a plan for a getaway car, but with this short notice, she is planning a daring foot escape. That is, until she realizes Gloria will be visiting. RoRo sneaks to the prison library, where she works five days a week, and on the "Do Not Circulate: Reserve Shelf," where she secured *Harry Potter and the Order of the Phoenix* for her own personal future use, she opens the classic to page 688, where her knife is hidden, in anticipation of a day like today. She just didn't know who would be at the other end of the knife. She hadn't even known of Gloria's existence before last week when Tarly announced that she was finally having a visitor, and she was a ghost hunter.

What Tarly didn't confide in her comrades was that Gloria was her husband's pen pal during his end days, and she was as curious as hell to know what he had to tell her. That was the trade-off: Boss's deathbed secrets for Lallie's deathbed secrets. But things change rapidly here at Bedford and Gloria would prove to be a great hostage, the deadly trio believed.

Yale's Hewitt Quadrangle is bustling today.

The second of the four presidential debates is to be held in Woolsey Hall tonight. The campus is lousy with photographers, cameramen, reporters, political wonks and politicians. Marcus is happily ensconced in his office, awaiting his visit from Gloria. An objective academic, he is surprisingly open-minded to Gloria's ghost theories. He would put nothing past Lallie. Plus, too many unexplained phenomena have occurred to him over the years since his conviction overturn and release from prison for him to doubt that Lallie was still seeking revenge. The mysterious death of his pets, the unexplained revisions in his doctoral dissertation, the green lights that would turn red as he drove through them. Gloria, he thought, might just be able to provide some answers.

After marrying Defense Attorney a year after he finally gained his freedom, she encouraged him to consider the legal profession. As someone who has seen the darkest side of the penal system, he would be more sensitive to the nuances of law enforcement and the court system. He agreed and reapplied to Yale. He was accepted and he and Defense Attorney moved to New Haven, where they have resided ever since. After graduating Yale's law school first in his class, Marcus was invited to apply for a tenure-track position where he would teach "Criminal Law" and "Evidence" courses.

Marcus loves his job. Mentoring the inquisitive minds that inhabit his venerable lecture halls is what drives him, and the pay isn't bad. He and Defense Attorney are unable to have children, so they have adopted three special-needs kids. They are Marcus' life. Thirty years ago, in the depths of despair frustratingly declaring his innocence, he could never, in his wildest imagination, have dreamed this idyllic life he now leads.

He and Defense Attorney have adjoining offices (she teaches the "Advanced Worker and Immigrant Rights Advocacy Clinic" and "Power, Responsibility, and Protection in International Humanitarian Law" course), and share lunchtime together. After winning her big case for Marcus decades ago, Defense Attorney decided to turn her attention to the plight of immigrants. Being a Dreamer, herself, it was a natural evolution, and a meaningful, personal calling. She has become one of the top immigration rights lawyers in the country and has already won two cases she successfully argued before the Supreme Court, winning landmark decisions in both. Between their professional and private family lives, their world is full. With Lallie back in their lives, through this meeting with Gloria, it's a difficult decision to make, but they both agreed it would at least be interesting, if not cathartic.

Marcus finishes off a scheduling meeting with one of his favorite students. Gloria's appointment is next. He waits, and waits, and waits. No Gloria.

Of course, there's no Gloria. She has a knife to her neck and she's driving RoRo, Mitchie and Tarly to RoRo's brother's house in Oklahoma City, 1,500 miles from their former cells.

"I have an appointment today," she says, after 20 hours on the road. "Can I cancel it?"

"No," snaps Mitchie, who's discovered Candy Crush on Gloria's phone and making up for lost time playing it.

Tarly, sitting in the backseat of Gloria's rented Camry, is looking forward to some private time with Gloria to discuss Boss once they get to Oklahoma City.

"I think Lallie's haunting me," she blurts out.

Mitchie laughs. "Why wouldn't she be?"

RoRo, dozing off next to Tarly, joins in the laughter.

"Could be," says Gloria. "I believe she's a ghost."

"No shit?" says Tarly.

"No shit," snaps Gloria, agitated about missing her meeting with Marcus.

"And how does she do that?" asks Tarly, worried.

"There's something about that apartment. 688. Her apartment. It's the number."

"Her apartment made her a ghost?" RoRo snarls, incredulously.

"I think so. My cousin, he discovered…"

The car suddenly, curiously loses control, and they crash into a guardrail on I-44. Mitchie is knocked unconscious from the impact. Tarly and RoRo, not wearing seatbelts, fly into the windshield. Gloria, a bit breathless from the airbag impacting her chest, feebly exits the smoky wreckage and waves down a state trooper.

Girlfriend has been on parole for five years, after spending a ten-year sentence she still doesn't accept.

She didn't think hiring a hitman would bring her so much time. It's not like she actually killed Bill.

On disability because of her mangled foot, part-time cashiering at Target is the perfect job. Bernadette helped Girlfriend secure the job, which enabled her to get parole and move in with her. Bernadette's house was large enough and she always had a warm spot for Girlfriend, her favorite and most troubled cousin. Bernadette kept a scrapbook of Girlfriend's modeling triumphs, but she keeps it hidden. Girlfriend wants nothing to do with her past. Bernadette also hid the letter from Gloria. There's no way she's opening that Pandora's box.

During lunch break, Girlfriend opens the tabloid on the table, and skims it. On page 5, there's a story about Defense Attorney taking on Daveed's case. Josefina was a household name years ago, and with the attempted deportation of her father, her story is now being revived. Girlfriend shakes her head reading that Josefina put off Tulane to help find her father who's gone missing. Is he in Guatemala? Was he killed there? No one's talking.

The fact is, no one really knows. Except for Garrett and Gloria. They have him well hidden and are not passing on information about his whereabouts until his case is resolved. ICE is certainly not going to discuss the case, because he was lost in their charge. Henry Epstor has been involuntarily retired and has taken to amateur ghost hunting. He believes his ghost is a former nanny who died in childbirth, after keeping her pregnancy a secret from her employers, the husband of which being the father. In Philadelphia, in a small café on Chestnut street, Carlisle, the hitman, is reading the very same tabloid, while waiting to meet a businessman who wants his partner offed. During the 20 years at this work, for some reason even Carlisle can't explain, Bill was the only intended hit he ever warned.

Gloria, recovering from the Oklahoma car crash and frightening kidnapping, is lying in bed checking off names of everyone she needed to interview. Not hearing back from Girlfriend was really no surprise, and being the last name on her list, she sets her paperwork aside and turns to Garrett and says, "We have to go next door. We have to figure it out."

Garrett is busily attempting to order tickets online for the new Live Aid benefit concert for Immigration Rights, to be held at the brand-new, open-air America Arena in Houston.

"Damn, this website is difficult to navigate," he complains.

"Give them a break. It's their first show, there'll be glitches," Gloria assures him.

"Got it!" he shouts. "Tickets DD667 and 668. Awesome."

"Garrett, we have to talk to Laura. We have to convince her to let us hunt in her apartment."

"We've been trying. She wants nothing to do with it. She's trying to forget what happened. You can't blame her. She's never really been fully absolved."

"I get it. I can't blame her, but something has to be going on next door. If our equipment is going berserk here, imagine what is happening inside her apartment. It's been the center of my attention forever, and I've never been there."

Garrett laughs, "It's like if Columbus never made it to America."

Gloria jumps up and laughs, "Yes, it's just like that." She plops down on the bed again and gives Garrett a prolonged kiss.

"Ahem," they hear at their bedroom door. It's bare-chested Daveed, who's been their secret house guest since the party. "Any word?"

Gloria explains that Defense Attorney believes that her negotiation with the government will conclude by Saturday. Daveed will retain his citizenship, although Guatemala has suddenly decided to gain some international attention by demanding his return. The family's entire journey has been an embarrassment to Guatemala, and they hope it might curry special favor from America's corrupt, anti-immigrant, executive branch.

Daveed smiles, gives a thumbs up, and when he turns, Gloria, again, admires Emma Lazarus' "The New Colossus" tattoo on his back.

LAURA

Gloria has been in all sorts of situations, but being surrounded by the freaks in Wretched Ray's was, at the least, disconcerting.

Ever since Ray's death, Laura has been rekindling her friendships with her circus friends, and they have become the most visible denizens of the bar. Todd Luft, who was always fonder of Laura than he was of Ray, was happy to welcome her back into the fold, and he remained her biggest benefactor when she was regarded as the prime suspect in Ray's death. He financially supported her over the two years she was officially under suspicion for the murder, but the case was eventually dropped because there was no other evidence than her being in the apartment. Somewhat gun-shy from the previous murder in that apartment, police were not about to jump to any obvious conclusions. Perhaps Wretched Ray committed a copycat murder and knocked himself unconscious, accidentally ending his life Lallie-style. But then there was that little thing about his head on the pillow. There was no forensic proof that Laura did it, even though it still appears that she would be the most likely candidate, abused and the only one admitting to being present. But no proof, no charges.

"Ugh," Gloria grunted, "Can't they see Lallie is behind this?"

"Tell them," Xavier would often tell her.

"I can't. They'll think I'm crazy."

Laura returned to the circus for a while, but decided, instead, to try to revive business at Wretched Ray's. And she was successful. She married Todd Luft a year and a half after Ray's murder, and Laura kept the apartment as an art studio. She was always a talented artist, but Ray always discouraged it. Returning to it was liberating. She and Todd lived on the upper West Side, with a view of Central Park. The circus was doing very well.

Laura was able to pick out Gloria right away. The startled look on her face, no piercings or tattoos; her wholesome aura gave her away. Ironic, since Laura, herself, appeared as plain as day, a far cry from the painted S&M circus queen of the past.

"Gloria?"

"Yeah, hi. Thanks for meeting with me, Laura. I know you've been through a lot, and the last thing you want is to revisit the past…"

"No, actually, Gloria, I've been giving it some thought, and I think maybe you can help me resolve some unanswered questions from the past." Laura looks around, and with a sweeping hand gesture, she says, "As you can see, I'm pretty open-minded."

Gloria releases some anxiety and laughs a bit too hard, "Yeah, I see."

"What is it exactly you want from me?"

Gloria is beside herself. This could be the beginning of the culmination of everything she's been working toward. She wants to pick her words carefully.

"I think there's a malevolent ghost in your apartment. I believe your apartment has been pre-destined for this kind of activity. It all has to do with mystical numbers, which I can explain to you sometime, but the most important thing is I think Lallie is alive in some form in that apartment and I would like to capture that with my high-tech equipment if it's all right with you." Yeah, she sure spit that all out.

Laura harrumphs. Staring, shaking her head, "Do you think Lallie killed Ray?"

Gloria doesn't even have to think. "Yes."

"And you think you can document all this with all your Ghostbustery stuff?"

Gloria can take a joke. Chuckling, "Yes!"

"Go for it, girlfriend," Laura replies, holding her palm up for a high-five. Gloria's so excited she hits Laura's hand so hard they both spin on their barstools.

"Want a drink, honey?" Laura asks, laughing.

"Sure do."

"Greg," Laura calls to the bartender who sports two medium-gauge side-cheek piercings.

"I'll have a red wine, and what about you, doll?"

"Bourbon Manhattan. Double."

"Got it," says Greg.

"So, Gloria, when?"

"Tomorrow night?" Gloria demurs.

"Got it. I'll leave the key with Greg. Don't mess up my artwork. Is it dangerous what you're doing?"

"We'll know tomorrow, I guess," says a wistful, but determined, Gloria.

RUSH OF RHYME

Gloria's trying to piece it all together.

She's desperate to make contact with the Otherside. She knows deep within her soul (she believes in that, too) that there's another plane. We just don't see it. She works hard trying to find it.

Giving sales pitch after sales pitch is tiring. Carrying her ghost-hunting instruments from house to house is burdensome. Holding on to one's beliefs is exhausting. Hearing a tone, a moan, a cry for help, watching meter levels rise and fall, lights flicker; she is never really sure deep down in that soul that she believes in, if it's actually real or if, as her father told her more times than she can remember, "Waste of time, Glory. It's an embarrassment to the family." The fact that she performs on Broadway doesn't mitigate her family's disappointment in her.

She looks at her wall-to-wall evidence chart. She knows that anyone who sees it other than the few (Xavier, Jackie, Garrett) she's trusted enough, would think she's out of her mind. She's seen enough *Criminal Minds* and *Homeland* episodes to know how to make these evidence maps. Colored strings binding connections, photos, quotes from her interviews, even a separate list, "Animals:" Joey Tribianni, Sheldon, Arya, Weasley, Sniggles, Bingos 1 and 2, King Kong and his siblings, Marcellus, Princess Meghan, and Admiral Jackson. What do they know? They've witnessed so much. Are their spirits waiting to come through and if so, would she be able to decipher the meanings of their messages? *Yes, I am crazy*, Gloria concedes.

Gloria's immersed in facts, sounds, lights, sensations, wonder and belief. *What does it all mean*? Why can't this rest like any other murder? Why do the pulses of these people, these strangers, to whom she's invested so much time and energy, beat, beat, beat so profoundly in her head? Why does she dream about Lallie? Why does she think she sees Stan on the street? Is that Boss driving the bus? Tarly serving her at Carmelito's? Why does Daveed's handsome, deeply lined face and grey temples haunt her? Is that the tinkling of Jenny's little-girl fingers on the piano she hears as she's drifting to sleep? Is Invisible watching her? Why does Matty Lynn, who she never knew, resonate so deeply?

Gloria rises from her desk, goes to the evidence wall, plucks the green string connecting the Sessameanys to Lallie, and walks to her computer, turns on Spotify, and plays Matty Lynn's "Rush of Rhyme." It's been omnipresent since Matty Lynn's death, and posthumously won that year's Grammy "Song of the Year" and "Record of the Year."

"When we're left here in the dark.
When the arrow hits its mark.
It can lead you to the light.
That tender tap you know is right.
…It's the hush and rush of rhyme.
The yin and yang of our lives.

"While we're walking through the stark.
Shadows shade all that is marked.
But a voice tracks through the crack.
And in its shine, we're pulled right back.
…It's the hush and rush of rhyme.
The yin and yang of our lives.

"Love's a mountain or a cloud.
Hard to see what's all around.
It's a feather or a weight.
It comes in time or it's too late.
...It's the hush and rush of rhyme.
The yin and yang of our lives.

"It's the tug and test of time.
That sweet quest that makes us right.
Echo echo of each climb.
To find the love we left behind.
...It's the hush and rush of rhyme.
The yin and yang of our lives.

"Can be destined or it's fate.
May be real or a mistake.
Talk and talk but we don't hear.

Let's vow we'll walk where there's no fear.
...It's the hush and rush of time.
The yin and yang of our lives."

There's life around us that we don't see. It's what love is. What challenges are.

Triumphs. Death. It's what is all around us. The good, the bad. The yin, the yang. The victim,

the crime. Time. The truth, the lie. The rhyme that we are. That apartment.

It is all the Invisible.

Excitement was definitely in the air.

Gloria couldn't sleep. Garrett couldn't sleep. Even Laura was restless. After Gloria left Wretched Ray's, a sudden neighborhood blackout added energy to the bar, with the freaks making the best of it, doubling up on drink and food orders. Who needed the jukebox when they could all sing? "Old Town Road," the #1 song for the past 10 years was the obvious singalong of the night.

Gloria and Garrett tossed and turned all night. No air conditioning, the windows remained open and the sounds of the street alternately lulled them to sleep and startled them out of their dreams.

As morning breaks, electricity returns and Gloria and Garrett check their gear. And check it again. All batteries charged, all equipment triple-examined. They sit in silence and quiet meditation until 7 p.m.

Garrett walks Gloria into Wretched Ray's and if someone were to be carefully observing, they would notice the indiscernible pull of everyone's bodies and stares (and piercings!) toward the perfect human magnet that was Garrett. He is causing more electrical interference than the previous night's blackout. He triggers a scene as the barroom hushes and the circus folk lick their lips.

Greg waves Gloria over and hands her the key.

"Good luck," he says.

"Thanks," Gloria replies, holding the key as if it were her lifeblood. She and Garrett return to their building, pick up their equipment from Gloria's apartment and walk next door, a 15-foot trek that seems endless. They stand in front of SI-E-GH.

"Here goes," they say in unison, and grasp each other's hands. Gloria takes the key and opens the door, just the way Lallie, Boss, Bill, Matty Lynn, Doctor, the Sessameanys, Wretched Ray and Laura had. The way the coroner had, the EMTs, the police. The way Little Theresa had on days she babysat for Garrett.

As they enter, Garrett instinctively turns on the kitchen light. He's overcome by rushing childhood memories.

Gloria sets up the equipment in the living room. Everything's operating properly. She and Garrett put on their Spectracles and turn off the lights. On the GhostBox, they hear a scratchy noise. Garrett gasps. He knows that sound. It's Invisible.

"Trouble's coming."

Garrett tells Gloria, "I can't do this, hon. I gotta get out of here."

"Really?"

"Really." He removes his goggles and leaves, hyperventilating.

He returns to Gloria's apartment, where Daveed asks him if he's OK.

"I'll be fine."

"What about Gloria? You left her alone?"

"Yeah," Garrett replies, still panting, guzzling water.

"I'm going over there," says Daveed, and he leaves in a flash.

He enters 688, and in the dark he sees all the equipment buzzing, and purring, and scratching. Static, hums, moans, cries, screeches, keening. The hair on his neck rises.

"You OK?" he mouths to Gloria. She nods, "Yes."

The lights turn on. Daveed turns them off. The kitchen faucet runs. Gloria turns it off.

The lights turn on again. The faucet pours again. The easel in the den falls. Daveed picks it up and returns the painting to the easel, an unfinished portrait of a sword swallower and a circus ringmaster holding a giant scarlet heart.

A kitchen chair grinds against the tile floor. Daveed is frozen to the ground. He's sending desperate telepathic messages to Gloria, *Vamos a salir de aquí,* but she doesn't respond. She, herself, is frozen.

The truth is, she's a fraud. She, like Fox Mulder, wants desperately to believe, but she has never actually heard or seen or has ever witnessed any evidence of a ghost.

But now?

"It's the Otherside," Gloria gasps.

The lights flicker wildly, as does most of their equipment. That scratchy noise that so scared Garrett is getting louder on the Portal BlackOut amplifier and it's being transcribed on the Gyrascope Digital Talking Board as "Trouble's coming."

"Oh, my g-g-god," Gloria stutters out loud. "It's… I-I-It's…"

"Gloria, look at this!" Daveed yells out, pointing to the laser grid.

On the screen, seen sitting on the couch, is a smiling, robust-looking Matty Lynn, the sunshine, and behind her, a barely discernible, indistinguishable mass that must be Invisible.

Lallie, the storm.

ABOUT THE AUTHOR

ROBBIE WOLIVER's books include *Wyoming & March* (New Directions in Education reading text); multi-media *Country Music Fancyclopedia*; *Bringing It All Back Home* (Random House/Pantheon) reprinted as *Hoot!* (St. Martin's Press); New York Times Bestseller, Independent Book Publisher's "Outstanding Book of the Year" and Oprah Library Selection *If I Knew Then* (iUniverse/HarperCollins); *Creation: A Novel* (iUniverse); and the award-winning, bestselling *Alphabet Kids: A Guide to Developmental, Neurobiological and Psychological Disorders for Parents and Professionals* (Jessica Kingsley Publishers/Hachette). His award-winning news writing was featured in *Best Alt Writing 2009/2010* (Northwestern University Press).

Robbie is a multi-award-winning journalist and editor who was a columnist and feature writer at *Newsday,* senior editor at the *Village Voice's* suburban edition, feature writer for *The New York Times*; and editor-in-chief of the alternative newsweekly *Long Island Press*. His freelance writing was published in *Rolling Stone, Village Voice, Demand Studios/eHow, San Francisco Chronicle, American Demographics Magazine, BankRate, Salon, Country Weekly, CBS MarketWatch, New York Post, Psychology Today and MSN.* Robbie is a recipient of the prestigious Casey Medal for Meritorious Journalism.

Before becoming a journalist and author, Robbie owned the venerable Greenwich Village music venue, Folk City, with his wife, Marilyn Lash, and they created and directed the National Music Awards, which included The New York Music Awards, L.A. Music Awards and Atlanta Music Awards, and helped coordinate the Boston Music Awards. They were co-producers of "Folk City: 25th Anniversary Concert" and its Halcyon Days video and PBS special.

Robbie is an award-winning playwright, whose theatrical adaptation of his book *Bringing It All Back Home—Folk City: The Musical*—won ten 2018 Broadway World Awards, including "Best Musical."

For the past eight years, Robbie has been a journalism and advanced-writing professor at New York State University College at Farmingdale and most recently he has been teaching at the University of Florida's School of Journalism.

Made in the USA
Middletown, DE
07 May 2020